"Why Do You Keep
Every Man Who Wants
In Me At Arm's Length?"

Kirby asked James again.

Oh, yeah. That. "Um..." he began eloquently. "It's because, ah... Well, you see..."

But try as he might to answer the question, James realized he simply could not. So what did Kirby do? She asked him another one.

"Because wasn't the whole point to find a man who would fall in love with me forever-after?" she began again, evidently unwilling to let it go until he gave her an explanation for his behavior.

He really wished he had one to offer her. Or to himself, for that matter....

Dear Reader,

This month Silhouette Desire brings you six brand-new, emotional and sensual novels by some of the bestselling— and most beloved—authors in the romance genre.
Cait London continues her hugely popular miniseries THE TALLCHIEFS with *The Seduction of Fiona Tallchief,* April's MAN OF THE MONTH. Next, Elizabeth Bevarly concludes her BLAME IT ON BOB series with *The Virgin and the Vagabond.* And when a socialite confesses her virginity to a cowboy, she just might be *Taken by a Texan,* in Lass Small's THE KEEPERS OF TEXAS miniseries.

Plus, we have Maureen Child's *Maternity Bride, The Cowboy and the Calendar Girl,* the last in the OPPOSITES ATTRACT series by Nancy Martin, and Kathryn Taylor's tale of domesticating an office-bound hunk in *Taming the Tycoon.*

I hope you enjoy all six of Silhouette Desire's selections this month—and every month!

Regards,

Melissa Senate

Senior Editor
Silhouette Books

Please address questions and book requests to:
Silhouette Reader Service
U.S.: 3010 Walden Ave., P.O. Box 1325, Buffalo, NY 14269
Canadian: P.O. Box 609, Fort Erie, Ont. L2A 5X3

ELIZABETH BEVARLY

THE VIRGIN AND THE VAGABOND

SILHOUETTE *Desire*®
Published by Silhouette Books
America's Publisher of Contemporary Romance

SILHOUETTE BOOKS

ISBN 0-373-76136-8

THE VIRGIN AND THE VAGABOND

ELIZABETH BEVARLY

is an honors graduate of the University of Louisville and achieved her dream of writing full-time before she even turned thirty! At heart, she is also an avid voyager who once helped navigate a friend's thirty-five-foot sailboat across the Bermuda Triangle. "I really love to travel," says this self-avowed beach bum. "To me, it's the best education a person can give to herself." Her dream is to one day have her own sailboat, a beautifully renovated older model forty-two footer, and to enjoy the freedom and tranquillity seafaring can bring. Elizabeth likes to think she has a lot in common with the characters she creates, people who know love and life go hand in hand. And she's getting some firsthand experience with motherhood, as well—she and her husband welcomed their firstborn, a son, three years ago.

For Aunt Sissy,
who thinks my books are way too racy.
I hope you like this one, too.

Prologue

"**I**'m saving myself for marriage."

Fifteen-year-old Kirby Connaught uttered the words without even thinking about them, such a staple of her vocabulary had they become. Then, with an angelic, self-satisfied smile, she forked a huge bite of potato salad into her mouth and chewed with much gusto.

Her friend Angie Ellison, who sat across from her at the picnic table in Goldenrod Park, rolled her eyes heavenward. "Well, duh," she replied eloquently. She fished a pickle spear from the Tupperware container near her hand and crunched it loudly. "Tell us something we don't already know, Kirb."

Rosemary March, who completed the trio of tenth-grade friends enjoying the sunny September afternoon, had perched herself atop the table with her sandal-clad feet flat on the bench beside Angie. "Yeah, Kirby," she said over her shoulder. "It's not like this is news to anyone."

"It is to Stewart Hogan," Kirby muttered, gazing suspiciously at the blond-haired, blue-eyed senior a few picnic tables down.

"When we went out the other night, you wouldn't believe what he wanted to do."

Angie and Rosemary exchanged knowing, wistful little smiles that made Kirby's face flush with heat. Her two friends had been dating since they were thirteen, and both had steady boyfriends now. And Kirby was vicariously familiar with all the things that went on with teenage courtship—the arms around each other, the hands in each other's back pockets, the hugging, the kissing, the necking.

She was sure her friends thought she was the biggest prude in the world because she never dated at all—the only reason Stewart had asked her out was because he'd just moved to town a few weeks earlier and didn't know about her spotless reputation that kept most of the boys at bay.

But Kirby's lack of experience with the opposite sex had nothing to do with a code of morality or a cold disposition. On the contrary, she often lay awake at night wondering what it would be like to do the things she longed to do with a boy, tried to imagine the feel of a boy's mouth and hands on her body, fantasized about experiencing for real all the scandalous things she'd read about in her favorite books by Anya Seton and Kathleen Woodiwiss and Erica Jong.

And when she finally did fall asleep, Kirby was often plagued by the most feverish dreams, dreams that left her feeling empty and achy upon waking. Despite what her friends—and everyone else in Endicott, Indiana—thought about her, she had a perfectly healthy adolescent libido and an equally healthy adolescent sexual curiosity. But she wanted to make sure it was the real thing with a guy before she went too far. Or anywhere at all, for that matter. Simply put, she wanted to be in love. Maybe that made her old-fashioned, but it certainly didn't make her a prude.

"Yeah, but Stewart Hogan just moved here," Angie said with a shrug, bringing Kirby's attention back to the conversation at hand. "He doesn't realize what a nice girl you are. Give him a few weeks of seeing you in action. Then he'll leave you alone. Just like all the other guys in Endicott do."

Rosemary chuckled. "Yeah, one look at you in your Cadet Scout uniform or your candy-striper outfit ought to cool any ideas he might have about taking liberties with you. And when he finds out you're president of Future Homemakers of America, he'll run screaming in the other direction.''

''There's nothing wrong with wanting to be a homemaker,'' Kirby stated crisply.

''I never said there was,'' Rosemary pointed out. ''But what guy wants to think about starting a family when he's only seventeen years old?''

''Don't worry, Kirby,'' Angie interjected. ''You'll find the right guy for husband and father someday. I think it's great that you're planning to wait for him.''

''Yeah, you're a braver man than me,'' Rosemary agreed.

Kirby smiled, but something deep inside her felt shut up tight. She was confident that the man of her dreams was out there in the world somewhere. She just wondered what it was going to take to bring him to a little nothing-ever-happens-here town like Endicott, Indiana.

The three girls, like everyone else who called the small town home, had turned out for the traditional Parsec Picnic in the Park, an official event that was part of the Welcome Back, Bob Comet Festival. Comet Bob actually had a much more formal, much more comet-appropriate name, but because everyone outside the scientific community was pretty much incapable of pronouncing the word *Bobrzynyckolonycki* unless they were three sheets to the wind, the name had been shortened some time ago to simply *Bob*.

And because Bob was such a habitual visitor to the skies directly above Endicott, the small southern Indiana town had come to claim him as their own. Despite the fact that it was unheard of for a comet to be so down-to-the-minute regular—speaking both in terms of time and of longitude and latitude—Comet Bob was exactly and unscientifically that. Every fifteen years, like clockwork, the comet returned to the earth during the month of September. And when it did, it always made its closest pass to the planet right above Endicott.

Hence the Comet Festival, which had been occurring in town every fifteenth September since the end of the nineteenth century. For whatever reason, Bob behaved with a regularity and predictability that had puzzled the scientific community since the comet's discovery nearly two hundred years ago. Furthermore, because of Bob's mysterious behavior, the comet had become something of a mythical being, in and of itself.

And as was the case with mythical beings, much folklore had grown up around Bob as a result. A lot of people in town said the comet's return to the planet made for a host of strange behaviors in Endicott. Put simply, people acted funny whenever Bob came around. Otherwise normal, functional folks would suddenly become…well, abnormal and dysfunctional. Elderly matrons donned leather miniskirts. Grunge teenagers became big fans of Wayne Newton. Husbands offered to do the cooking. Very odd behavior all around. And, too often for it to be ignored, people who would normally dismiss each other without a glance, fell utterly and irrevocably in love.

And then, of course, for those who liked their folklore to be magical, there was the myth of the wishes.

It was widely believed by the Endicotians that people who were born in town during the year of the comet had a distinct advantage over those who were not. It was said that if a native Endicotian's birth occurred in a year of Bob's appearance, and if that person made a wish during Bob's next visit, while the comet was passing directly overhead, then that person's wish would come true when Bob came around again.

Kirby, Rosemary and Angie had all been born the year Bob had made his last visit. And two nights before, as the girls had lain in the soft, green grass of Angie's backyard, each had sent a wish skyward while the comet was making its closest pass to the planet.

Angie, Kirby recalled with a smile, had wished for something exciting to happen in the small town. It was a fitting wish for someone who exaggerated everything and saw spectacles where there were none, simply to spice up an otherwise mundane, mediocre, midwestern life. Kirby, however, would be satisfied if Endicott never changed. She liked the slow pace and predictability. It was the perfect place to settle down and raise a family.

Rosemary, she recalled further, her smile broadening, had wished that, someday, her thirteen-year-old lab partner, a pizza-faced little twerp named Willis Random, would get what was coming to him. Another appropriate wish, Kirby thought, seeing as how Willis and Rosemary were generally at each other's throats. But Kirby kind of liked Willis, even if he did have an IQ the size of the Milky Way and didn't let anyone ever forget it. There was something decent and lovable about him, something that would make him a good husband and father someday.

Kirby had made a wish that night, too, she reminisced as her smile grew dreamy. A wish she had made often for years. She'd asked Bob for true love, the kind that outlasted eternity. She wanted someday to find a man who would love her forever, a man she would love in return with all her heart. A man who would build a home with her, start a family with her, share her dreams and desires for all time. A forever-after kind of love. That was what Kirby had wished for.

And because she knew Bob had granted wishes before, and because hers was so very noble, Kirby was certain the comet would see fit to answer her prayers. Bob was constant, after all. Predictable. Dependable. Just like the man she hoped to find for herself someday.

Bob would grant her wish by the time he made his next approach to the planet—she was sure of it. By her thirtieth birthday, Kirby would be settled down, married with children and happier than she had ever imagined she could be. Of that she was completely confident. Because Bob, she knew, had never proved himself wrong.

Bob always made wishes come true.

One

Ah, September.

The blue skies and languid days. The stretches of sunny summer weather that made a person feel as if he were cheating the universe somehow by enjoying them. The subtle fusing of one season to another, as days shortened and nights grew longer almost seamlessly. The soft splashes of early-autumn color dashing the leaves of green. The quiet shift of the wind from warm to cool and back again as it whispered over one's face.

The golden, burnished glow on the skin of naked sunbathers.

James Nash trained his telescope not on a heavenly body up in the sky, but on one that was nestled on a chaise longue. A chaise longue in a backyard he estimated was a little over a mile away from the twelfth-story hotel suite where he'd set up his makeshift observatory. Providence had surprised him with the magnificent view as he'd been surveying his temporary surroundings, and now he was making the best of it.

He'd been scoping out the area, so to speak, trying to get a feel—from a safe distance, naturally—for Endicott, Indiana, the small town that would be his home for the next few weeks. But now he found himself wanting to get a feel of something else entirely. And from considerably more close up.

Originally, the only reason he had come to this dinky little backwater town was to observe a comet, an opportunity he'd been awaiting since he was a little boy. Simply put, James loved comets. He was fascinated by their travels, by their legends, by their mystique. Comets never stopped moving. Never slowed down. Vagabonds, that's what they were. And he could really relate to that.

In fact, there was only one thing that James loved more than comets, and that was the feminine form. So he smiled as he shamelessly studied the naked woman who was enjoying the sunny afternoon the way God had intended. And he thanked his lucky stars that he had come by his massive fortune the old-fashioned way—by inheriting it—and not because he had a lot of money invested in useless things like privacy fences such as the one surrounding this particular feminine form's backyard.

She was a sight beyond celestial beauty, with a body whose perfection made James want to lift his voice in song. Lying on her belly with her face turned away, her hair caught atop her head in a spray of silver-white, she boasted a golden back and bottom, unspoiled by the telltale white of bikini interruption. And her legs... Aye, caramba. Her legs were long and lean and bronzed, quite possibly the most perfect legs he had ever seen in his life.

And James Conover Nash IV had seen a lot of female legs in his time, of virtually every nationality. Since skipping out ten years ago on a Harvard education he hadn't wanted in the first place, he'd trotted around the globe at least two dozen times.

And since his father's death six years ago, he'd had little reason to curb his activities. James III hadn't exactly been a monk by any stretch of the imagination. But even he, old hedonist that he had been, had tried while he was alive to put a leash on his son's ceaseless partying from continent to continent.

Out of respect for the old man, James IV had tried to be discreet in his debauchery. But since his father wasn't around to be embarrassed by his son any longer, James didn't bother to hide his many and sundry appetites. Instead, he fed them without inhibition, unconcerned that they regularly grew more voracious.

However, he wasn't thinking about all that right now. Right now, what he was thinking was that he'd really like to get to know those legs in that chaise longue better. And that bottom attached to them, too. And the back. The hair. Oh, what the hell. He wouldn't mind making the acquaintance of the entire woman.

"Begley!" he called out as he reluctantly pulled back from the telescope.

Before he'd even completed the summons, the valet he had also inherited from his father stood stiff and waiting beside him. "Yes, Master Nash?"

James squeezed his eyes shut and drove a restive hand through his shoulder-length black hair. "Would you please call me James?" he asked the ancient-looking man, as he did on a daily basis. "I'm thirty years old, for God's sake."

Instead of commenting, Begley sidestepped the request—as he always did—and asked, "What was it you required?"

"I'm going out."

The announcement was more monumental than it sounded, because James *never* went out in public. Not voluntarily, at any rate. And certainly not without a disguise. A man of his world-renowned celebrity couldn't afford to be seen among the masses, because those masses would good-naturedly rip him to shreds in search of a souvenir to recall the moment.

"And what shall you be wearing?" Begley asked.

At the moment, James wore nothing but a pair of pewter-color silk boxer shorts, accessorized with a cut-crystal tumbler of Scotch. So he thought for a moment, sipped his drink, then thought some more.

"The eggplant Hugo Boss, I think," he finally decided. "No, wait," he interjected as Begley turned toward the closet on the other side of the room. "This occasion calls for something more casual." He wiggled his dark brows playfully at the valet. "After all," he added, "the woman I'm going to see isn't wearing anything at all."

Begley's expression didn't waver. "May I suggest the Armani, then. The gray trousers and white…what I believe you Americans call a 'T'." He gritted his teeth as he concluded speaking, though James was too much of a gentleman to call him on it.

"Perfect," he replied with a smile. "The gray will match my eyes."

Begley arched a single snowy eyebrow. "Quite."

As the elderly valet went to collect James's wardrobe, James himself turned back to the telescope that remained trained on the naked blonde. Her face was still turned away from him, but she had arced an arm above her head and stretched her toes to pointe, as if she were a prima ballerina executing a pirouette. Something inside James tightened fiercely, and he felt himself stirring to life.

"Down, boy," he instructed a particular part of his anatomy that suddenly seemed to defy his control. "There will be time enough for that later. Lots and lots of time, if I have anything to say about it."

And of course, he was certain that he would. It was easy for James to make assumptions about women, because all women invariably reacted to him exactly the same way. They fell recklessly and utterly in love with him, often for weeks at a time. There was absolutely no reason for him to think that the woman at the other end of his telescope would behave any differently.

"Shall I have Omar bring the car around?" Begley asked from the other side of the room.

James nodded, a smile curling his lips. "Most definitely," he told his valet.

"And what shall I tell him is your destination?"

Reluctantly James shifted the telescope until he located a street sign two houses down from the one where the woman lay sunbathing. "Tell him we'll be visiting a pink stucco house near the corner of...Oak Street and...Maple Street." He turned to Begley with another smile, then downed the rest of his Scotch. "Isn't that great? Oak and Maple streets. Is this midwestern stuff quaint, or what?"

Begley arched that single white brow once again. "Quaint. Quite. I shall telephone Omar immediately."

"Yeah, do that. Tell him I'll be down in fifteen minutes." With one final glimpse through the lens at the sunbathing beauty, James turned toward the clothes Begley had laid out on the king-size bed. "And tell him to bring a book with him. *War and Peace*, maybe. Because I'm planning on being a while."

* * *

Kirby Connaught was teetering on the precipice of unconsciousness, enjoying the sensation of the warm sunlight soaking into her bare skin, when the hair on the back of her neck leapt to attention. She snapped her eyes open wide. How odd. She'd had the strangest sensation that someone was watching her. But that was impossible. The eight-foot, privacy fence surrounding her backyard was impenetrable. And besides, her neighbors on all sides were at work.

She would have been at work herself, if she'd had any work to do. Unfortunately, she was quickly discovering that trying to get a business off the ground in a small town was next to impossible. Especially when that business involved something like interior decorating.

Simply put, no one in Endicott, Indiana, wanted change. Ever. Not to their small-town culture, not to their small-town values, not to their small-town economy. And not to their small-town homes, either, evidently. Nothing ever happened in the tiny community, anyway, so why should anyone be amenable to change? Kirby would probably be more successful trying to launch a career as a voodoo queen.

There had been a time in her life when Kirby had loved her hometown for the very reason that it did resist change and development. She'd liked the quiet pace, the simple pleasures. She'd wanted nothing more than to marry a local boy, settle down and start a family here. In fact, she still wanted those things. Which was probably why Endicott was starting to annoy her so much lately. There were reminders everywhere of all the things she had wanted and hadn't been able to find.

She closed her eyes again, but couldn't quite shake the sensation of being watched—and very intently, at that. Nonsense, she tried to tell herself. The only way anyone could be watching her would be if they were on the roof of the Admiralty Inn, the tallest building in town, a good mile away. And even if someone were watching her from that lofty standpoint, she'd just be a smudge of chaise longue amid a sea of grass. No one would be able to tell that she was naked. No one in Endicott had *ever* seen her naked.

Not that she hadn't tried.

In fact, Kirby had spent the last two years of her life trying to get naked with men, but no man in Endicott had ever been even remotely interested in getting to know her that intimately. She was the town good girl—too nice, too sweet, too innocent, too virginal for anyone of the male persuasion to even attempt to try *that* with her.

But then, she had no one but herself to blame. She'd always chosen the path of goodness—had been the most highly decorated Girl Scout, the most conscientious candy-striper, the perkiest cheerleader, the most dependable baby-sitter. And after her father's death when she was twelve, she had become the sole caretaker for her mother, who had been weakened by heart disease shortly after Kirby was born.

Everyone had considered her a saint after that, even though Kirby had just thought herself a daughter who loved her mother. And when her mother passed away shortly after Kirby's eighteenth birthday, the entire town had turned out in sympathy. After that, Endicott had, in effect, become Kirby's caretakers. Older folks became surrogate parents. Younger folks became surrogate siblings. And no man in town wanted to get intimate with his sister.

Too, when Kirby had become old enough to understand what sex was all about, she'd insisted on saving herself for marriage. Of course, now that she was thirty years old and a potential life mate was nowhere to be found, she had altered her philosophy on that in a number of respects. Two years ago, as a matter of fact, shortly after her twenty-eighth birthday, when she'd realized that thirty—and Bob's next visit—were so near on the horizon.

It had occurred to her then that if she was going to find that forever-after kind of love she'd wished for when she was fifteen, by the time the comet made its next visit, then she was going to have to give Bob a little help.

Unfortunately, by the time she began to rethink her virginal status, most of the eligible men in Endicott had been claimed— a good many of them by women who hadn't shared Kirby's opinions where their own maidenhead had been concerned. What few available men were left simply didn't view Kirby in a particularly sexual light. Not that any of the others had felt any differently.

She sighed heavily, thought about moving someplace where no one knew her, then, as always, dismissed the idea completely. Endicott was her home, the only place she'd ever known. Although she had no family left to speak of, her friends were here. She'd never traveled as a child, and simply had no desire to move. The thought of starting up all alone somewhere just held no appeal.

So she lived in the house where she had grown up, existed on a small income from investments, struggled to make her decorating business a viable source of income and spent most of her time alone.

She opened one eye and gazed up at the cloudless, pale blue sky. "Thanks for nothing, Bob," she muttered.

Darned comet. So much for the myth of the wishes. So far, Bob was zero for three. Angie's excitement had yet to materialize, Rosemary's lab partner had yet to get what was coming to him and Kirby was nowhere near finding a forever-after kind of love. Endicott was still boring, Willis Random—if you could believe the gossip—was thriving as a brilliant astrophysicist teaching at MIT and not one single example of husband-and-father material had come close to entering Kirby's orbit.

"Some wish-granting comet you turned out to be," she added morosely, closing her eye again.

But when she heard what sounded like the faint *ding-dong* of her front doorbell singing through the soft silence of the backyard, she jumped up from the chaise longue and thrust her arms through the sleeves of a short peach-colored kimono, then dashed into the house.

"I'm coming!" she shouted as the doorbell sounded impatiently several more times. "Will you please lighten up on that thing? I'm not deaf," she concluded as she jerked the door open.

"No, what you are is incredible."

The rich, masculine voice poured over her like something hot, liquid and sticky. For a moment, Kirby could say nothing in response to the man's observation, so surprised was she by his appearance on her doorstep. So she only gazed at him in silence, mouth slightly agape, wondering if she hadn't simply fallen asleep on the chaise longue and been plunged into one of those erotic dreams that plagued her from time to time.

Her guest was, in a word, gorgeous. His jet-black hair, sleek and straight, was bound at his nape in a ponytail by some currently invisible means of support. A white short-sleeved T-shirt, deceptive in its simplicity and clearly not Fruit of the Loom, loosely covered—but not quite loosely enough—a torso corded with muscles. The baggy, pale gray trousers were also obviously of expensive cut, cinched around a slim waist, trim hips and legs she would have killed to know more about.

But what caught her attention most was the single, exquisite, apricot-colored rose the man held in one hand, and the dewy magnum of champagne he held in the other. Quickly she forced her focus back to his face, where her surprise at his appearance had prevented her gaze from lingering. Now she took in his features, one by beautiful one, and felt the world drop away from beneath her.

His eyes were as pale as his hair was dark, an almost mystical gray framed by long, sooty lashes and straight, elegant black brows. His nose was narrow, his lips full and his cheekbones had evidently been carved from Italian marble. As she watched, his magnificent mouth curled into a smile, and he tipped his head forward in greeting.

"Hello," he said simply.

When Kirby realized her mouth was still hanging open, she quickly snapped it shut. "Uh, hi," she began eloquently.

He smiled a mischievous little smile. "My name's James. What's yours?"

"Kirby," she replied without thinking.

"Wanna come out to play?"

She blinked at him three times quickly, as if a too-bright flash had gone off right in front of her eyes. "Wh-what?" she stammered.

He shrugged. "Okay. We can stay in and play. I'd like that better anyway."

She shook her head hard in an effort to clear it of the muzziness that had overtaken it, and wondered if maybe she had spent too much time in the sun. Behind the beautiful man who stood on her front porch, everything appeared to be the same. The yellow chrysanthemums she'd planted along the walkway were starting to bloom, a few early fallen leaves were scattered about her impeccably groomed yard, and there was still a pothole at the foot of her driveway that she was going to have to call the city about seeing to again. Nothing at all out of the ordinary.

Except, of course, for the silvery Rolls-Royce, complete with liveried driver behind the wheel, that was parked at the curb in front of her house. That was certainly something she didn't see everyday.

She turned her attention back to her unexpected visitor. "Who *are* you?" she managed to ask.

His smile fell some, as if he couldn't quite believe she had just posed the question she had uttered. "Who am I?" he repeated. He expelled a single, incredulous sound. "I'm James Nash."

Kirby said nothing, waiting for him to elaborate. But when he only stood there gazing at her, she added, "What are you selling?"

His beautiful eyes nearly bugged out of his head at her question. "Selling? What am I *selling?*"

She nodded, gripping the front door more tightly, ready to close it tight. It didn't matter how good-looking this guy was or that he had been ferried by Rolls to her front door. She was tired, she had a headache and she was in no mood for fun and games.

She remembered then that she was also naked under her robe, and the thought of fun and games suddenly took on a more sinister connotation. Certainly Endicott was one of the safest places on the planet by national standards, the kind of town people normally only chose to visit by sticking a pin in a map. Then again, there were a lot of weirdos out there who could stick a mean pin.

"Whatever you're selling," Kirby said as she began to push the front door closed, "I don't want any."

Before door met jamb, however, her visitor stuck the toe of his obviously expensive, clearly Italian, loafer in the opening, effectively interrupting the brush-off. A thrill of something slightly scary shivered up her spine, and Kirby tried to push harder.

"You don't understand—I'm James Nash," the man repeated

slowly and clearly, as if he were speaking to a two-year-old child. "Nash," he said again. He paused a moment before adding, "You might have seen my face on the cover of *Tattle Tales* magazine a few months ago. They've designated me the Most Desirable Man in America this year."

Although Kirby could certainly believe a man who looked like he did was capable of winning such a distinction, she didn't for a moment put credence in his claim. "Um, congratulations," she said as smoothly as she could. "But you evidently have me mistaken for the Most Gullible Woman in America." Without missing a beat, she added, "That would be my friend, Angie. She lives on the other side of town. Now if you'll excuse me... Goodbye."

She tried again to close the door, but the man who called himself James Nash, Most Desirable Man in America, kept his foot firmly planted between it and the latch. And he smiled again, looking devastating and yes, darn it, desirable. She frowned as a spark of heat sputtered to life in her midsection. Boy, she really was desperate for a man if a total stranger was flicking her Bic.

"You really don't know who I am?" he asked. "You honestly don't recognize my name?"

Kirby sighed impatiently, chanced opening the door wider and said, "No. Sorry. Should I?"

He chuckled with genuine delight. "You've really never seen me before?"

She shook her head.

"Not on TV? In magazines? On the Internet?" He leaned forward and lowered his voice conspiratorially as he added, "I'm a regular weekly feature on the show, 'Undercover Camera'—it's syndicated, so you'll have to check your local listings—and there's an entire web site dedicated to sightings of me. If you'd like, I can write down the URL for you."

Kirby paused, utterly bewildered by what the man was telling her, but reluctantly entranced by his deep, resonant voice. When she finally regained her senses—what few of them she could collect—she shook her head again. "Sorry," she repeated. "But I have no idea who you are."

He gazed at her in silence, as if he weren't quite sure of her species origin. Then a shimmer of amusement lit his eyes. "How utterly delightful," he murmured. His smile turned dazzling as he ran a hand modestly over his hair. "Think a minute. Surely you've heard my name somewhere. James Nash. I'm an icon of popular American culture."

Kirby smiled back—indulgently, she hoped, because one could never be too careful when one was confronted by mental instability. "Well, gee, I guess that would explain it," she said carefully. "I'm not much of a fan of popular American culture. I don't own a television or have access to the Internet, and the only magazines I read are related to the decorating industry."

"There you go," he said with a nod. "Two of my houses were featured in *Architectural Digest* last year. And *Metropolitan Home*'s latest holiday issue was practically devoted to my Central Park condo."

Kirby nibbled her lip thoughtfully for a moment as she searched through the files in her brain. She eyed the man more carefully. "Don't tell me that leopard-print sofa and zebra-striped club chair were yours."

He beamed. "You remember!"

"And *you* need a new decorator," she said, making a face. "I hated that spread."

His smile fell. "But I love that sofa."

This time when she shook her head, it was with a cluck of disapproval. "Look, that whole African explorer thing went out a long time ago. Today's decorators are getting back to the basics. Doing more with less. Simple lines, clean colors. Lots of light and space. Not dead animals."

His expression was crestfallen. "But I like dead animals."

"Hey, guy, so did Ernest Hemingway, but that didn't make him an expert in interior design."

She suddenly remembered that she was standing at her front door wearing little more than a suntan, jawing with a man of indeterminate psychological status about home furnishings. With the hand she didn't have wrapped around the doorknob in a white-knuckled grip, she clutched more tightly the top of her robe.

"Um, look," she tried again, "it was, uh, nice, um, meeting you, Mr., ah...Nash, was it?"

He nodded, his dashing smile returning full-blown. "Please...call me James."

"Okay. Goodbye, James. I really have to go." And she tried, again without success, to push the front door closed.

He gazed at her through the Italian-loafer-wide opening in the door, as if he couldn't believe what she'd just told him. "Go?" he echoed. "But I just got here."

She arched her eyebrows silently at his announcement.

"I brought champagne," he added, holding up the bottle of what even she, with her very limited knowledge of such things, could see was extremely expensive wine.

Still not quite certain that she wasn't dreaming the entire episode, Kirby said softly, "I don't understand what that has to do with anything."

"I brought champagne," he repeated in that voice of put-upon patience, as if she should know exactly what he intended by the statement.

"And that would mean...what?"

His lips curled once more into that devastating smile that kindled a quick fire in her belly. "It means that by the time we finish dinner this evening, we'll both be feeling pretty frisky."

The fire in her belly exploded at that, sending flaming debris all through her system. She told herself he couldn't possibly be intimating what he seemed to be intimating. He couldn't possibly be intimating that they should get drunk and get...well, intimate. Was he?

"Um," she began. But she couldn't make herself say more than that.

James evidently interpreted her lack of response as the positive reply he seemed to be expecting, because that twinkle of something scandalous came back into his eyes. "You don't even have to change your clothes," he said softly. "It just so happens that my favorite outfit for a woman is nudity. Especially when there's no tan line to act as an unnecessary accessory."

Kirby gaped at that, because she suddenly realized that her earlier sensation of being watched while sunbathing had been founded after all. She didn't know how "Mr. Desirable" Nash had managed it, but now some man in Endicott had finally seen her naked. And she hadn't even had to try.

"What?" she said, the odd encounter becoming more and more surreal with every passing moment.

He nodded, smiling, obviously not noticing her growing fury. "Don't worry," he said softly. "I won't tell your neighbors what a hedonist you are. And I don't know if you realize it or not, but sunbathing nude is rivaled only by one thing in pleasure." He winked lasciviously. "Sunbathing nude with a friend."

He held up the bottle, now sweaty with condensation, and the sight of the moisture streaking down its sides wreaked havoc with something dark and dangerous inside her that she immediately tried to tamp down. But still, Kirby was unable to utter a sound.

So James continued blithely. "Well, sunbathing nude with a friend and a big bottle of champagne. You just never know where the combination of the two might lead you." He dipped his head forward and wiggled his eyebrows suggestively. "But wouldn't it be fun to find out?"

Instinct told her to slam the door as hard as she could and hopefully break at least one of his toes. Reason told her to scream at the top of her lungs and hope that one of her neighbors dialed 911. But ultimately Kirby did neither of those things.

Instead, with one swift move, she snaked a hand out the door, grabbed the bottle of champagne, and then pushed James Nash as hard as she could. It wasn't hard enough to send him sprawling onto his fanny, as she had hoped, but she surprised him enough to knock him off balance, forcing him to remove his foot from the door. When he did, she slammed the door tight, bolted it and slid the chain into place.

Then she opened the six-inch-by-four-inch door-in-a-door that served as her peephole and told him, "Thanks, Mr. Nash, but I think the champagne will suffice very nicely on its own."

And with that, she slammed the little door on him, too, and left him standing there bemused, and gorgeous—not to mention all alone—on her front porch.

James could only gape in disbelief at the sight of the big wooden door so close to his nose. A woman had actually slammed the door in his face. *Two* doors, if he counted the little one, too. *And* she'd stolen his champagne. An entire magnum. Of Perrier-Jouët.

That meant war.

Outraged, he lifted his fist to knock again, then hesitated when a startling realization smacked him right upside his head.

This was a new experience.

After all his years of globe-trotting and debauchery, he had begun to think there were no new experiences left for him to enjoy. He had embraced Been There, Done That as his motto long before it had been silk-screened onto T-shirts for mass consumption. He had indeed been virtually everywhere in the world, and he had done virtually everything there was to do.

African safari? Circumnavigating the globe? Done that. A visit with the Dalai Lama? Tea with the Queen of England? Done that. Slept in the Blue Room at the White House? Yawn. Done that, too. Seen Siegfried and Roy perform? Done that twice. It was all a big crashing bore by now. For years he'd been convinced that there simply was, for him, no such thing as a new experience.

Yet this Kirby person was presenting him with exactly that. Not only was she absolutely clueless as to his identity and notoriety—something with which James had *never* been confronted—but she seemed in no way interested to learn more about him. Women *always* knew who he was. And they *always* wanted to get to know him better.

There were women out there who had actually formed a club, the members of which made it their sole purpose in life to sleep with him. They even had special little badges available to award to those who succeeded in their quest—*if* they succeeded.

Not that James approved of such a single-minded goal. People should have some hobbies, after all. And in spite of all the sordid stories printed and broadcast about him, he was nowhere near as promiscuous as the tabloids and trash TV made him out to be. Oh, sure, he loved women to distraction, but he wasn't totally without standards. He never involved himself with women who were on the rebound. He avoided women under the age of twenty-one. And he certainly steered clear of married women.

Still, he did like women. Very much.

His gaze skittered to the mailbox, a tidy little brass rectangle, embossed with a tidy little frog on a tidy little lily pad, and tidy little letters proclaiming the property as 231 Oak Street. And just below that, more tidy little letters spelling out the name Connaught. Kirby Connaught, he mused further. It shouldn't be too difficult to uncover the secrets of her life. This was small-town America, after all, right?

Clearly he had a full afternoon ahead of him. Or, at least, Begley did. There was no way James could go out on a fishing expedition himself—he'd be netted and scaled in no time flat.

When he realized he still held the perfect, apricot-colored rose in his hand, he lifted it to his nose for an idle sniff, its tangy, sweet aroma filling his senses. He tucked it into Kirby's tidy little mailbox and spun on his heel to leave, awed by the episode that had just transpired.

A new experience. How very extraordinary.

A blond, blue-eyed beauty who'd had no idea who he was had slammed the door right in his face. A door on a neat little pink stucco house, sitting on nothing less than Oak Street, U.S.A. A pink stucco house that had a frog on its mailbox and yellow flowers sprouting along the walk.

James shook his head in wonder. Kirby Connaught was about as small-town, middle-American a woman as he could conjure up in his wildest dreams, the epitome of all that baseball-and-Mom-and-apple-pie mentality.

Except for that naked sunbathing business, he thought further, something he *really* wanted to investigate more thoroughly. Her enjoyment of such an activity suggested that beneath the delectable exterior of this small-town girl there was a hedonist's soul to rival his own just begging to break free. Now all James had to do was make her realize the true nature of her inner self.

But then, he was the Most Desirable Man in America, he reminded himself in matter-of-fact terms, without a trace of arrogance. And no woman could resist that for long. Not even a small-town, middle-American one who lived in a tidy little pink stucco house, right?

Smiling, James spun around toward his waiting car, feeling more purpose than he'd felt in a long, long time. A new experience, he marveled again. A true adventure. Kirby Connaught, he decided resolutely, was going to provide him with both.

Kirby peeked through the curtains of her living room window, and observed with what she assured herself was only idle interest the departure of James Nash, icon of popular American culture.

What a jerk, she thought. Acting as if he need only show up at her front door to have her fall to her knees and beg him to make love to her. Obviously he was unaware of her high standards where men were concerned. Clearly he had no idea that she was only interested in men who were decent and warm and conscientious, not to mention local. What would she possibly want with the likes of James Nash?

Other than hours of unbridled physical satisfaction, of course. She squeezed her eyes shut tight to banish the uncharacteristic idea that leapt to life in her brain. Unfortunately, closing her eyes only brought the graphic images into stark focus.

She really had gone far too long without experiencing the sexual satisfaction any normal human being required, she thought with a sigh that sounded disturbingly wistful. All her life she had saved herself for the perfect union, and now that perfect union seemed well beyond her reach. No man in Endicott was interested. The way things looked now, she was going to end her days as a dried-up old spinster, a local legend for every young girl to whisper about, and for every young boy to fall back on in efforts of seduction.

Better be careful, they'd tell their would-be conquests. *Or you might end up like Old Lady Connaught, who at ninety years of age has never even come close to enjoying the Big O.*

Kirby sighed wistfully again, not even trying to deny the fact that she was just that—wistful. If she was so worried about winding up a shriveled old virgin, and if she knew she would never find the perfect match, then why couldn't she be satisfied with an imperfect one? she asked herself, not for the first time. Why hadn't she just jumped at James Nash's more-than-obvious offer?

Immediately she knew the answer to that question. Because deep down, she still harbored some small hope that Bob would bring her a man who would love her forever after. And she wanted it to be special when that man appeared. James Nash, she was certain, wasn't that man.

Even if he'd been telling the truth about making the cover of *Tattle Tales* magazine—which, of course, she sincerely doubted—he was far too caught up in himself to ever give a woman any kind of attention. And if he *was* a celebrity—again, something Kirby suspected was a complete fabrication—then that was all the more reason for her to avoid him. Because there was no way any celebrities would ever settle down and start a family in Endicott.

The sound of his car rumbling to life outside brought her attention to the window again, and something inside her trembled in time with the purr of the Rolls's engine. Through the sheer curtains, she watched as the silvery car pulled slowly away from the curb. And for some reason, the only thought that tumbled through her head was that her very last chance was slipping right out of her grasp.

She shoved the odd idea away and headed for her shower, determined not to give another thought to James Nash. It wasn't like she didn't have enough to keep her mind occupied for the next few weeks, anyway. She was, after all, serving on the committee of the Welcome Back, Bob Comet Festival, something that would keep her unusually busy for the month of September. She had a million things to organize, a million events to oversee, a million places to go, a million people to meet. She had a comet to welcome back. Whether Bob was bringing her a wish come true or not.

Two

A few hours later, she was feeling fresh and clean, dressed in a loose, white cotton sheath with three-quarter sleeves, a wide, scooped neck and sailor-type collar. But better than that, she thought as she strode into the Endicott Free Public Library to meet with the other festival committee members, she had gone a whole half hour without a single vision of James Nash erupting in her brain.

Upon entering the cavernous marble structure, however, her gaze was drawn to the periodicals section to the left of the checkout desk, and her thirty-minute record was broken. Darn. All she could think about then was that with a brief, effortless investigation, she could easily verify James's claim to worldwide notoriety and nationwide desirability.

Glancing down at her watch, Kirby found, not much to her surprise, that she was fifteen minutes early for the meeting. She was always early for functions. Simply because, by virtue of her less-than-thriving business and completely inactive social life, she was pretty much overcome by leisure time.

Without thinking about her motives, she strode casually toward the periodicals, her white flats scuffing softly along the marble floor. She scanned the shelves until she located the one where *Tattle Tales* magazine just so happened to be housed, then thumbed nonchalantly through the last few months' worth of issues, until she located one whose cover carried a very familiar face.

Good heavens, he'd actually been telling the truth. His name really was James Nash, and he really had been dubbed the Most Desirable Man in America.

Her brain lurched into overdrive, but Kirby somehow managed to steer herself slowly to a nearby chair and park herself in it. Then she gazed dumbfounded at the magazine's cover, a full-face photograph of the man who had stood on the other side of her front door just a few hours ago.

Naughty Nash! the headlines beside his name screeched in big red letters. Then, in smaller type, was the added sentiment But Oh...So Nice!

Chiding herself for being genuinely curious about the man, Kirby flipped through the magazine until she located the story about him. Another photograph of his beautiful face assaulted her senses, and that odd sparkle of heat fired to life in her belly again.

"Playboy, paladin, parasite, pariah," the article began. "They're all words that have been awarded to this year's Most Desirable Man in America. Whatever. Regardless of his rough reputation, one thing nobody can deny about James Nash is this: he's plain perfection."

Well, my goodness, it sounds like someone's been nipping at the alliteration juice again, Kirby thought uncharitably about the article's author.

Then, unable to break her gaze from the other words on the page, she continued to read. "He's wonderfully wealthy. He's incredibly intelligent. He's appealingly adventurous. He's gallantly gorgeous. And, of course, he's sensuously sexy. What more could a woman desire in a man?"

Gosh, Kirby thought to herself, *maybe stalwart stability. Obeisant honor. Absolute affection. That sort of thing. Oh, but, hey, as long as he's really rich and fabulously famous...* She shook her head morosely and read further.

"James Nash has seen all, done all, dated all. He's been linked romantically with royalty and riches, glamour and glitz, fashion and fame, celebrity and sass. He has a string of relationships in his past, yet not a single one of his former loves has a negative word to say about him.

"'Every woman should have a man like James at least once in her life,' stated starlet Ashley Evanston in a recent telephone interview. Debutante Sissy Devane, daughter of billionaire Russell Devane, concurred. 'No man is more knowledgeable about what it takes to please a woman,' she said with a little purr of delight this author couldn't mistake. 'James is quite thorough in his sexual technique.'"

Oh, please, Kirby thought, slamming the magazine shut. Was nothing sacred? Why did people air their sex lives for public consumption as if they were sharing recipes?

She told herself to simply toss the magazine back on the shelf where she'd found it and forget about the fact that James Nash had ever darkened her door. But for some reason, she just couldn't quite put the man to rest.

She supposed there was really nothing wrong with reading the article, she told herself. Just so she'd know what she was up against should James Nash decide to come around again, of course. With a quick glance over her shoulder, she tucked the magazine between herself and her purse, then hastily made her way to the check-out desk and placed it on the counter.

On the other side, Mrs. Winslow, who had been senior librarian since Kirby was a child, smiled as she rose from her desk. "Good evening, Kirby," she said in that even, quiet librarian's voice as she approached, tucking a pencil into the snowy bun atop her head.

Kirby forced a smile in return and tried to pretend she really couldn't care less about the item she had chosen to check out. "Hi, Mrs. Winslow."

"I see the festival committee is meeting upstairs tonight. Big plans this year?"

"Oh, you bet."

"Did you ever find someone to replace Rufus Laidlaw as grand marshal of the Parallax Parade?"

Kirby shook her head. "Not yet."

"Well, it's going to be hard to find someone of Rufus's caliber," the librarian said with a certain nod. "There aren't many people in Endicott who've achieved such celebrity status."

"No, ma'am. You're right about that. Not many people from here have costarred in laxative commercials, that's for sure."

"And don't forget the one where he played a dancing can of corn."

"Oh, I could never forget that. It's a shame he had to cancel, even if that cancellation came because of a boost to his career. But don't worry. We'll find someone."

"I'm sure you will." Then Mrs. Winslow glanced down at Kirby's choice of reading material and made a soft *tsk*ing noise. "I'm sorry, dear, but periodicals don't circulate."

Kirby arched her eyebrows in surprise. "They don't?"

The librarian shook her head. "That's why we have the reading room over there. Of course, there are those who prefer to photocopy the articles they wish to read. Be aware, however, that should you do so, you might potentially be violating copyright law."

"Oh, I wouldn't want to do that," Kirby assured Mrs. Winslow. "I have a few minutes before the meeting. I'll just go to the reading room."

Mrs. Winslow smiled, clearly satisfied that Kirby had made the right moral choice.

Kirby spun around, her attention drawn to the picture of the man staring at her from the magazine cover. The glossy paper James's smile was as flirtatious as the real life one's had been, and his eyes in the photo held all the mischief she had seen in them in person. She supposed a man like him could turn the charm on and off like a faucet, adjusting the flow and temperature in accordance to whether or not there were flashing cameras and/ or his adoring public within range.

So caught up had she become in studying the smiling, handsome face on the magazine's cover, that it came as a tremendous surprise to her when a familiar, masculine voice said out of nowhere, "Then again, why would you want to photocopy the thing when you can have the genuine article?"

Kirby snapped her head up at the question, only to find herself falling into the depths of those pale gray eyes that had so captivated her earlier. James Nash had changed his clothes, too, she noted, and now wore charcoal trousers, a white, open-collared shirt with the sleeves rolled to just below his elbows, and a knit black vest. His jet hair was still bound at his nape, and for some reason, she found herself wondering just how long it was.

"What are you doing here?" she asked, hoping she only imagined the husky, breathless quality her voice seemed to have adopted.

"Following you," he told her frankly.

The tremor that had begun in her belly when she first saw him began to rattle throughout her entire body at the ease with which he offered his statement. "Why?" she managed to ask.

He shrugged casually, as if his answer should be obvious. Then he took a few idle steps toward her, his gaze never leaving hers. "Because wherever you were going, I wanted to go there with you."

"Why?" she repeated.

He smiled as he halted a few inches shy of her. "Because I'm *very* curious to learn more about you."

"Why?"

His smile grew broader. "What are you? Generation Why?" he mimicked. "I should think the answers to all your questions would be obvious."

"Well, they're not."

This time he was the one to inquire, "Why?"

Because no man has ever been in the slightest bit interested in finding out where I was going, she wanted to shout at him. *Because no man has ever been curious to learn more about me, that's why.* Instead of answering him, however, Kirby remained silent.

He sighed with what she could only interpret as disappointment. "Whatever. You know, for some reason, to see you go scuttling up the steps of the local library was in no way surprising."

"What's that supposed to mean?" she demanded, finally finding her voice.

He met her gaze levelly. "Just that after what I've learned today, I shouldn't be surprised that you would indulge in such quiet, safe activities, that's all."

Kirby narrowed her eyes at him. "And what's *that* supposed to mean?"

Instead of answering her directly, he said, "You know, most people wouldn't feel guilty about reading something like *Tattle Tales* magazine—its circulation is huge. And most people sure wouldn't feel compelled to hide it under their purse as they carried it up to the check-out desk."

She gaped at him, fighting off a blush, burning inside that he had been observing her as she read about him. "I did *not* hide it under my purse."

He chuckled, a sound that was soft, certain and seductive. "Like hell you didn't."

"Mr. Nash—"

"Please, Kirby, I thought we'd gotten past that. Call me James. After all, I have seen you naked."

Even without turning around to look at her, Kirby knew Mrs. Winslow's head snapped up at that pronouncement. She knew, because she heard the little gasp of horror that accompanied it. Kirby closed her eyes tight and tried to rein in her mortification.

"Only because you're a...a...a promiscuous...playboy... Peeping Tom," she declared through gritted teeth.

She spun around to look at the librarian. "Mrs. Winslow, he didn't really...I mean, he and I didn't... What I mean is, I would *never*... Especially with someone like... You know my reputation in town is..." She halted suddenly when she realized she was making absolutely no sense.

But Mrs. Winslow only raised a steady hand, palm out, and shook her head. "You owe me no explanation," she said. "Bob has been officially sighted out there in the cosmos, and we can't be held responsible for our behavior once the comet is within range. Whatever you do in your spare time now, no one can fault you."

"But I'm not doing anything in my spare time," Kirby insisted. "Least of all...*that*. Especially not with someone like...*him*."

"Whatever you say, dear." Unfortunately, the librarian didn't look at all convinced.

"Honest," Kirby reiterated. "He was spying on me."

"Kirby, don't be embarrassed," Mrs. Winslow continued. "I myself have even succumbed to the comet's influence. Last night, I went to the Videoramajama, intending to rent a Jane Austen double feature, and came home with two Keanu Reeves movies instead. And they were actually quite good. He's a rather remarkable actor, even without a shirt." She paused a thoughtful moment then added, "Yes, indeed I would venture to say that shirtless, he is without question in his milieu."

And with that, Mrs. Winslow dropped her gaze back to the assortment of colored index cards littering her desk and continued with her task.

Great, Kirby thought. She supposed she should feel thankful that no one other than Mrs. Winslow had overheard James's comment. The librarian was one of the few people in town who frowned upon idle gossip. Then again, whatever was going on between her and James felt anything but idle. She lifted a hand to her forehead and rubbed ineffectually at a headache she felt threatening. Then she spun back around to face her accuser.

"Let's get a couple of things straight right now," she told him.

He smiled. "Gladly."

She took a few steps forward, lowering her voice as she drew nearer. "Number one," she began slowly, "you did *not* see me naked."

James rocked back on his heels as his grin turned smug. "Oh, yes I did. And quite a sight it was, too."

"You didn't have my permission to look, therefore, it doesn't count." Then, before he could protest, she held the copy of *Tattle Tales* aloft and hurried on. "Number two, I did *not* pick up this magazine because there was an article about you in it."

Now his grin turned *really* smug. "Oh, no?"

"No," she assured him. She lifted the magazine up for his inspection and pointed to a small box in the upper right hand corner. "See this? There's an article about Joe Piscopo in here. Now, I don't know about you, but I've always been a big, *big* fan of Joe Piscopo."

"Have you now?"

"Oh, yeah. I used to have a cat named Joe."

"Do tell."

"And that's not all," she continued, riffling through the pages until she came to the back of the journal. She scanned the columns fiercely, then thrust her finger against the first ad she saw. "Just look at this."

Nash bent forward, squinting to see what she was pointing at. "What?" he finally asked.

"It's an ad for...for..." She, too, turned her attention to the magazine, then swallowed hard when she realized what she had selected by chance. She tried to make her certainty convincing as she said, "An ad for...um...ThighMaster. And I...uh...I really need one of those."

His expression was impassive. "Really? You'd never know it to look at you. And if you'll recall, I have looked at you. Thoroughly." As she fought off another blush, he bent forward and extended his hand toward the hem of her dress. As he did so, he added playfully, "But I suppose, if you insist, it wouldn't hurt to have another look."

Viciously she smacked at his hand just before it made contact. "Mr. Nash," she began again.

"James," he interjected, jerking his hand out of the way.

She ignored the distinction and instead continued. "I don't know why you keep bothering me, but I assure you I—"

"I'll be more than happy to explain it to you," he interrupted her. "Over dinner. In my suite. Tonight. How about it?"

She emitted a brief, quiet sound of disbelief. "I don't think so," she stated emphatically. "Now if you'll excuse me, I have an appointment."

"That's okay. I'll wait." This time he reached for the magazine. "I can read all about my nationally desirable status."

Instead of handing over the magazine that still dangled from her fingers, Kirby snapped it shut and spun on her heel toward the stacks where she'd found it. As she went, she threw a comment over her shoulder. "I'd advise against it."

James followed close behind, his step perfectly aligned to hers. "Against reading about myself? Or against waiting for you?"

"Both."

"Why?"

"Because *you're* not all that interest*ing,* and *I'm* not at all interest*ed.* That's why."

"You might want to at least listen to my offer."

She glanced over at him hesitantly, felt that odd heat starting to unwind in her midsection again and quickly looked away. "Oh, I think you made it abundantly clear this afternoon what you were offering. And as I told you then—whatever it is you're selling, I don't want any."

"Who says I'm selling it?"

Before she tossed the magazine back down onto its shelf, Kirby held it up for his inspection. "It's all right here in black and white, illustrated in living color."

"That doesn't say I'm selling it," he argued. "On the contrary, that article only goes to describe what a very *giving* person I am."

She nodded. "Yeah, that's the problem. You give it to everything in a skirt."

"Not necessarily," he countered. "Sometimes they're wearing pants. Or swimsuits. Or wet suits. Or ski gear. Or lingerie. Or nothing at all."

Kirby wished he wouldn't go into such detail. She really didn't want to know. Mainly because it hurt to realize that the only reason he had any interest in her was because of her gender. He'd leap on anything that had produced estrogen at some point in its life.

"You don't have to spell it out for me," she muttered. "I know what kind of man you are. I know you've been with a lot of other women."

He smiled at her phrasing. "*Other* women?" he asked softly. "Why, Kirby, you almost sound like you're jealous."

She rolled her eyes and squelched the realization that for some bizarre reason, she was precisely that. "Oh, please. If there's one thing I'm not, it's jealous of anyone who might come into contact with you."

"Your lips say 'no,' but your eyes..."

He let the old adage drift off, his smile becoming so smug now that Kirby wanted to smack it right off his face. With no small effort, she prevented herself from tearing the magazine to shreds right before his eyes—it was, after all, library property—and instead slammed it back down onto its resting place.

"Go away," she said as clearly as she could. "Leave me alone. I never want to see you again."

He laughed, a low, rough sound that was more than a little suggestive. For some reason, she had the impression that he wanted to touch her. But instead of reaching out, he shoved his hands deep into his trouser pockets and continued to stare at her as if he couldn't quite believe she was real.

"You are *such* an interesting woman," he said softly, his voice a near purr. "So exciting. So stimulating. So..." He inhaled deeply and released the breath in a slow, ragged stream, as if he were trying very hard to rein in some impulse that threatened to gallop out of control. "So...arousing," he finally finished on an uneven whisper.

Well, that certainly caught Kirby's attention. In addition to having never been seen naked by any man in Endicott, she'd never been called exciting or stimulating—and certainly not *arousing*—by any man in Endicott. And she'd never been looked at as if she were some half-naked Venus to be plundered, either.

But with one heated look and a few suggestive remarks, James Nash seemed to be more than capable of making up for all the past oversights of every man in town. Kirby was suddenly assaulted by a sensation she'd never experienced before, a thrill of something hot and urgent and needful boiling up inside her, a hunger for some unknown quantity that only James Nash could fill.

Uh-oh.

"I...I...I..." she began. But for some reason, no other letters came forth to form words that might help her out of her predicament.

He moved a generous step forward, an action that brought his body to within inches of hers. Kirby felt as if his heat were surrounding her, and when she inhaled, she filled her lungs with the scent of him, something dark and masculine and exciting. His gaze fastened on her mouth, his lips parted slightly, as if he were about to bend forward and sweep her into oblivion.

And even though she assured herself that kissing a man like him was the absolute last thing she wanted to do, she realized a profound disappointment when he didn't kiss her.

Instead, he lifted one arm to prop it against the bookcase beside them, and leaned in farther still, until his face was scarcely millimeters away from hers. Kirby breathed deeply of him again, holding her breath inside for as long as she dared, growing dizzy and intoxicated by the scent of him. And when her eyes began to flutter downward, when she felt herself involuntarily drawing closer to him, she had to force herself to pull away.

She snapped her eyes open and exhaled unsteadily, willing her heart rate to level off. But her pulse only quickened when her gaze met James's. Because the way he was looking at her was downright scandalous.

"Have dinner with me tonight," he instructed her without an ounce of inquiry in his voice.

"I...I...I..." Kirby gave her brain a mental shove to drive it out of the scratched groove it had entered. Unfortunately, when she did that, she found that every instinct she possessed was insisting she shout "Okay!" in response to his demand.

With a fierce mental *shush* to her instincts, she said softly, reluctantly, "I can't."

Her refusal had no effect on him whatsoever. He only continued to gaze at her in that maddeningly seductive way and lifted a hand to her face. In an act of self-preservation, she ducked her head away from his touch. But he only curled his index finger gently beneath her chin and effortlessly nudged her head backward, until she found herself gazing into his face again.

Then, oh, so softly, he asked, "Why not?"

Her blood roared as it rushed through her body, its velocity striking heat in every cell it hurtled past. For a moment, she could only stare at him, wondering how on earth she had found herself in such a situation. She wanted to throw caution to the wind and take him up on anything—everything—he had to offer.

Then she reminded herself what kind of man he was. He didn't claim a single character trait she insisted upon finding in a mate. He was a ne'er-do-well with no marketable skills, no job, no formal education, no roots and no desire to settle down. Okay, he was rich, so he didn't really have any need of those particular traits, she conceded. Fine. He still wasn't the kind of man she needed or wanted.

"I...um, I have other plans," she stammered. "I have to be somewhere. Right...right now, as a matter of fact."

Still, he was unfazed by her assertion. He cupped her jaw resolutely in his warm, rough hand and skimmed his thumb lightly over her cheekbone, starting a fire deep inside her that she feared would rage on forever.

"Like I said," he told her softly, "I'll wait."

When he lifted his other hand, skimmed her hair aside and curved his fingers easily around her nape, her heart beat even more fiercely. "Oh..." she breathed softly, her eyes fluttering closed as the flames leapt higher and hotter inside her.

The thumb stroking her cheek continued its erotic rhythm as the fingers on her nape began to urge her forward, closer to James. For one delicious, delirious moment, she let herself be swayed, allowed herself to be overrun by his touch, his voice, his scent, his power.

Then, when she realized how easily she was succumbing to him, she forced her eyes open, leaned away and continued. "I mean, uh...I...I might be a while."

He smiled that sexy smile again, and his gray eyes grew dark with something that touched her way deep down inside her soul. "That's okay," he said softly. The thumb caressing her cheek shifted down to skim lightly over her lower lip, and a tiny explosion of delight sprayed against her belly. "I don't mind waiting for you," he added. "You're worth waiting for."

Oh, wow, Kirby thought.

This was definitely a new experience for her. No man had ever spoken to her in such a blatantly suggestive way before. But here was James, an absolutely gorgeous specimen of manhood, who was actually interested in her, who was actually coming on to her, who was actually trying to...to...oh, God, who was actually trying to *seduce* her.

Not him, she told herself. Anyone but him. He was the last man on earth she should go up against. Over and over she told herself these things, until finally, finally, the warnings registered in her flustered brain. And when she realized she stood so little chance against him, when she understood that as long as he was within a football field's length of her, she wouldn't be able to resist him, then she knew all she could do was try to escape.

"No!" she cried suddenly, doubling her fists against his chest to shove herself backward, stumbling away from him when she finally did. Involuntarily her hand flew to her mouth, the backs of her fingers rubbing lightly over the lips he had touched so tenderly. Though whether she was trying to wipe away the sensation of his caress or preserve it forever, she honestly didn't know.

Too late, she remembered that she and James were standing in a library. A really quiet library. A really quiet library with marble walls and floor, something she realized belatedly created a virtual soundstage for echoes. The moment the word *No!* left Kirby's mouth, it ricocheted right back at her, punctuated by the stunned expressions of a dozen people nearby, and Mrs. Winslow's fiercely uttered librarian's "Shush!"

When Kirby saw that the majority of the people staring at them were members of the festival committee on their way upstairs for the meeting, she dropped her head helplessly into her hands. Then, without another word, without a backward glance, without a single thought for how monumentally embarrassed—and how utterly turned on—she still was, she spun around and fled.

As James watched Kirby's flight, something he couldn't ever recall feeling before unfolded deep in his belly. Regret. Honest-to-goodness regret that he would be denied the pleasure of her company for even a short period of time. He'd never felt that way about anyone in his entire life. Not about his family—such as it was—nor his friends—such as they were—nor his companions—ditto—nor even his lovers—major ditto. Yet a simple blond woman who was nearly a complete stranger had made him feel exactly that. Regretful. Bereft. Alone.

Amazing.

Then again, he recalled, Kirby wasn't exactly a *complete* stranger. Not quite. Not anymore. Begley had discovered all kinds of things about her on his fishing expedition that afternoon, things that made James feel as if he knew her pretty well.

He shook his head in wonder as she disappeared through a pair of doors on the other side of the room, ahead of a group of people, all of whom—except Kirby—were glancing surreptitiously back over their shoulders at him. Only when they were completely out of sight did James allow himself to relax, to remember how soft and warm and compelling Kirby had been during their brief encounter, and to ponder again the wealth of information his valet had uncovered during a stroll through town a few hours earlier.

Begley had waxed poetic in particularly rhapsodic terms about an establishment dubbed the Dew Drop Inn, especially with regard to a certain proprietress named Jewel, of generous stature and even more generous proportions. In fact, Begley had gone on for so long about Jewel's many charms that James had begun to wonder if his valet had ever even gotten around to completing the errand on which he'd been sent. Namely, digging up as much dirt as he could on a local citizen named Kirby Connaught.

Fortunately, Begley being the trusted and reliable servant that he was, he had performed his duties admirably. Eventually. And Jewel, it appeared, had been the one to provide him with all the sordid details.

According to the local barkeep, Kirby Connaught was a very good girl, a local scion of all things morally decent and profoundly innocent. She never had a harsh word to say about anyone—except, evidently, James. Nor was she capable of even the slightest misbehavior—except, apparently, theft of expensive champagne.

She was an orphan of modest means who still lived in the pink stucco house where she'd grown up, but also a daring entrepreneur who was trying—with questionable success—to launch her own decorating business. She was a regular churchgoer, a passionate art lover, an avid gardener, a reliable volunteer. A former cheerleader. A former calendar girl. A former senior class secretary, candy-striper, Girl Scout and National Merit Scholarship Semifinalist.

And, word had it, she was also a virgin. And not a former virgin, either. A current one.

That last part had really thrown James for a loop. Surely it wasn't true. Surely the gossip was completely wrong. Surely there was no way the men in this town were stupid enough to have overlooked such a tempting, delectable, ripe, succulent, luscious, mouth-watering...

He inhaled a ragged breath and released it slowly. Such a supreme example of Venus in all her glory. Yet somehow, James knew that the gossip was indeed true. Kirby's responses had been too quick, too obvious, too sensitive, too artless to have come from anyone other than a virgin.

How could such a thing have happened?

Of course, there was always the possibility that Kirby herself was responsible for her untouched status, he thought further. Maybe she simply gave any man who approached her the brush-off. After all, hadn't she just done that very thing with him? She could be frigid, completely uninterested in sex. Or even a man-hater, for that matter.

Immediately, though, he knew that wasn't true. He could tell by the way she had responded to his touch only a few moments ago that she was in no way frigid. There was, without question, a wantonness in her that ran deep and strong. Kirby had a healthy sexual hunger—there was no question about that. What James couldn't figure out was why she tried so hard not to feed it.

He returned his attention to the copy of *Tattle Tales* that sat innocently on the shelf. Although he had shouldered the mantle of Most Desirable Man in America with some pride, he hadn't read the accompanying article in the magazine. Mainly because he honestly hadn't cared what it said. Not until he'd seen Kirby perusing it. Now he couldn't help but wonder what kind of conclusions she had been drawing as she read.

Probably none that were any worse than the ones she had already drawn about him, he thought dryly. For such a scion of innocence, purity and goodness, she sure was quick to see the worst in people.

Reluctantly he reached for the copy of the glossy tabloid and gazed at the picture of himself as indifferently as he could. Not the best shot that had ever been snapped of him, but it wasn't bad. The headlines, however, were a little extreme. He wasn't nearly naughty enough to warrant an exclamation point. Nor was he nice enough to have commanded an ellipsis. Not the way they meant it anyway.

He glanced up again at the door through which Kirby had passed with her colleagues. He had meant it when he'd told her she was worth waiting for. Folding himself into the chair she had vacated, oddly thrilled by the knowledge that his fanny was occupying the same cushion hers had, James sat himself down and began to read.

Three

Almost an hour after running away from James, Kirby exited the committee meeting, filled with both anticipation and dread. Part of her was praying that after their parting, he had become bored with whatever game he had initiated with her, and had abandoned both it and her to hunt for bigger game. But another—and if she were honest, a bigger—part of her was hoping like crazy that he was still in the library reading room waiting for her.

He was.

Lounging comfortably in the overstuffed, burgundy-colored chair she had occupied earlier, his long legs stretched out before him and crossed at the ankles, he had his head bent down over a magazine in his lap, his attention utterly focused on whatever he was reading. One elbow was propped on the arm of the chair, and his hand, with knuckles bent slightly, cradled his strong jaw. Kirby's gaze was drawn to the bare forearm exposed by the rolled-up sleeve of his shirt, and she wondered why she'd never noticed before just how sexy a man's arms could be.

And his hands, too. James Nash may be a globe-trotting celebrity, but he had great hands—big, bronzed, broad, blunt-fingered.

They looked like a laborer's hands, yet she was certain he'd never performed an honest day's work in his life. Sailing, perhaps, or mountain climbing maybe, or some other adventurous activity, must be what had given him such roughened, strong-looking hands and such a fit, well-formed body.

How would those hands feel caressing a woman's skin? she wondered out of nowhere, both shocked and fascinated by the idea. Then she realized she already knew the answer to the question. She had already felt his hands on her face, the rough tips of his fingers gliding over her cheek and neck and throat. But how would it feel to have his fingers skimming over other, more sensitive parts of her anatomy?

She felt herself coloring at the thought and banished it, assuring herself that she would never discover the answer to that question, because from here on out, she intended to maintain a very safe distance from James Nash. Then, in direct opposition to her resolution, she strode toward him with slow, hesitant strides.

It amazed her still that he had selected her for the focus of his attentions. Why? She had no idea. There were dozens of single women in Endicott, all of them far more capable than she was of handling a man like him. Why had he singled her out, especially after she'd made it clear to him that she wasn't interested?

Then again, she knew he had a reputation for being a little eccentric. She knew this, because the topic of the festival committee's discussion all evening had *not* been about the numerous festival issues facing them, but had instead focused on none other than James Nash, Kirby's new best friend.

Even after she'd assured the other members that she and James were anything but friends, that she'd only made his acquaintance that very afternoon—and under dubious circumstances, at best—everyone had insisted she should be the one to ask him the Big Question.

The Big Question being: Would he be interested in appearing as the grand marshal of the Parallax Parade, replacing the until-now irreplaceable Rufus Laidlaw, Hollywood wannabe?

The Big Question was, to Kirby's way of thinking, a Very Bad Idea, something that would force her to be in contact with him a lot more than she really wanted to be. Part of her position on the committee was seeing to out-of-town visitors, making them feel welcome, being sure they had everything they needed, presenting them with the absolute best view of Endicott that the small town had to offer.

PR—that was Kirby's main objective. But where James Nash was concerned, somehow the *P* in PR came to stand much more for *personal* relations than it did *public*.

She slowed her step as she drew nearer, wishing she could do something to stifle the shudder of electric heat that tried to overtake her every time she came within ten feet of him. But that little incident they'd shared in the library stacks a short time ago was still far too fresh in her memory for her to be able to banish any kind of trepidation she felt around him. On the contrary, seeing him again so soon after such an encounter only made her feel more wary, more cautious, more scared.

And alas, more turned on.

She told herself that she was merely the victim of her own libido. Any man who had said to her the things James had said, who had touched her the way he had, would make her overreact, simply because she'd never had a man speak to or touch her that way before. It wasn't James Nash specifically who caused her to feel so...so...so wanton, she decided. So needy. Goodness, so *hot*. It was the man's behavior, nothing more. Once the novelty of being treated like a sex kitten wore off, surely she'd see past his handsome, sexy, erotic, hot, uh...handsome exterior, to the promiscuous playboy Peeping Tom beneath.

As if he knew how she'd just labeled him, he lifted his head slowly from his reading material, then met her gaze with laughing eyes. She forced herself to look away and found herself staring at the copy of *Tattle Tales* unfolded in his lap.

When she stopped a few feet shy of him, he rose from his chair and carefully closed the magazine. "It's true," he said in a library-appropriate whisper. "You really can't believe everything you read. I had no idea there were so many errors in this article."

Kirby arched her eyebrows in surprise. "You mean you hadn't read it yet?"

James shook his head. "Nah. Why would I want to read about myself? I already know everything. It would be boring. I really don't care for nonfiction, anyway." He glared down at the magazine again. "Then again, seeing as how this article is almost complete *fiction,* you'd think I would have enjoyed it a bit more than I did."

She feigned shock. "What? You mean the press has succumbed to sensationalism? I had no idea. How very appalling."

"Sensationalism?" he echoed, her sarcasm evidently lost on him, so sharp was his anger. "Are you kidding? This is filled with flat-out lies."

Kirby, not sure whether to believe him or not, only adopted what she hoped was a bland expression and replied, "Really."

He nodded fiercely. "I mean, I can't believe Sissy Devane said what she did about me. She and I only dated for a week, and we *never* slept together."

"Oh, no?" Kirby asked dubiously.

James shook his head. "No way. She was never sober enough. And Ashley Evanston? Please. She's just a kid. I met her once in Telluride for all of thirty minutes. If she's posing as my former lover, and actually convincing a so-called journalist that we had a love relationship, then she should win an Academy Award this year."

Kirby eyed him skeptically. "So what you're saying is that your reputation with the ladies is undeserved?"

He smiled. "Well, no. I didn't say that. Just that my reputation with these two particular ladies—" he flipped the magazine open again "—and about a dozen others in this article—is."

Kirby couldn't resist moving alongside him, glancing around his arm at the article in question. She pointed to the highlighted box that took up a full one-third of the page, headed with the words James's Hit List So Far... "So this list of women they say you've slept with isn't exactly correct?" she asked.

He shook his head. "Of course not. Just look at this. They've got Princess Fatima listed, for God's sake. As if *any* man could get through *her* chastity belt."

Kirby gaped at him. "They still put princesses in chastity belts?" she asked, incredulous. She knew some of those eastern emirates were rough on women, but that seemed a bit archaic, even for contemporary archaic societies.

"It was a figure of speech," James told her. "In Fatima's case, the chastity belt in question is a huge linebacker of a woman, allegedly her secretary, named Lyudmila." He scanned the list of names again. "Wait a minute... Good God, they listed Lyudmila, too. And nearly every one of the Rockettes. Two. I dated two Rockettes and this is what happens."

Kirby couldn't believe she was standing in the Endicott Free Public Library with James Nash, calmly discussing the number and identity of his sexual conquests. It was maddening to realize that the innocent exchange they had shared earlier was of little consequence to him. To her, the encounter, however brief, had been one of a kind, unlike anything she'd ever experienced before, something she couldn't ever hope to recreate with someone else.

But for James, obviously, that kind of thing happened all the time. And with scores of women, too. She had been thinking that the way he'd touched her earlier had been something special. But for him, evidently, it had been no more unusual than changing his socks. She was handy right now, that was all. There was nothing at all special about her in his eyes. Any female who stood in the same room with him was likely to have him reacting the same way.

With a roughly uttered sound of derision, he closed the magazine and tossed it back onto the shelf. Then, turning his back on it, he looked at Kirby again. "Have dinner with me," he said, the request as insistent and as confidently offered as it had been earlier.

She told herself to refuse, that to promote or prolong any kind of contact between them would be pointless. Then the words of her colleagues on the festival committee resounded in her ears.

You obviously know James Nash very well, Kirby. I bet he'd say yes if you were the one inviting him to be the grand marshal of the Parallax Parade.... That had come from her third-grade teacher, Mrs. Dumont, her most favorite teacher in the whole wide world, who had offered the comment without even the slightest smirk of disapproval, much to Kirby's surprise.

Think of the national exposure we'd get from the press, Kirby. The international exposure for that matter.... That had been Mrs.

March, her friend Rosemary's mother, who also happened to be the mayor of Endicott.

He'd bring in an awful lot of people to festival functions, Kirby. And remember—a lot of the proceeds from the festival go to local charities.... Dr. Vanessa Brown, Kirby's former pediatrician and currently the chairwoman of the local children's hospital, which gained considerably from the money raised by festival events such as the parade, phrased the request that way.

It couldn't hurt to ask him, Kirby.... Mrs. Mankowicz, who had led Kirby's Girl Scout troop, and who now ran the local women's shelter, another establishment that received funds from the festival coffers, pleaded.

Please, Kirby? Pretty please...? Mayor March again.

All in all, it had been an awesome display of firepower coming from just about everyone who'd ever had an influence on her in the past.

No, she decided, it couldn't hurt to ask James to be the grand marshal of the Parallax Parade. Not unless he said yes, of course. In which case, it would hurt Kirby a lot.

She sighed in defeat, and before she even realized that she was going to do it, she heard herself say, "Okay. I need to ask you something anyway. It's kind of a favor."

His eyebrows shot up in surprise at that. "Really? You need a favor? From me?"

She nodded silently.

"Is it a very big favor?"

She nodded again.

He smiled at that, a smile she decided she didn't like one bit. "And if I say yes," he went on, "will you feel indebted to me?"

A minor hesitation, then another, slower, nod.

"Really, really indebted? Or just indebted? Because if it's a big favor, then I think you should feel really, really in—"

"James, please."

"Ooo, you're even saying please and being civil to me. It must be a *really, really, really* big favor, in which case, if I agree, you're going to feel *really, really, really* indebted."

She ignored his enthusiasm and said pointedly, "Dinner?"

His smiled softened some. "Why, Kirby, I thought you'd never ask."

How he talked her into joining him in his hotel suite, Kirby never did figure out. She supposed it was all that stuff about him being recognized and attacked and stripped naked by the general public the moment they entered a crowded restaurant that finally swayed her. The thought of James naked—regardless of how he'd gotten that way—was simply too troubling for her to imagine.

The reason for her capitulation certainly couldn't be because the man seated across from her at the candlelit table was more beautiful than any man she'd ever laid eyes on, she assured herself. Nor was it because, with a few simple words, gentle touches and heated glances, he had jump-started parts of her body she hadn't even been aware of owning before. And it certainly wasn't because, for the first time in her life, a man was making her feel like a woman to be enjoyed, instead of like a friend to be trusted, or a sister to be watched over, or a daughter to be protected, or a dandelion to be overlooked.

No. The reason Kirby was sitting in a half-lit room with James Nash, surrounded by soft music and freshly cut flowers, drinking mellow wine and eating cholesterol-heavy food, with her pulse rate doubling every time he looked at her, was really very noble. She was here with James only for the benefit of her hometown, and for the good people of Endicott. For the children's hospital. For the women's shelter. For the very preservation of the midwestern life-style they all embraced and cherished in southern Indiana. For...for...

For Pete's sake.

She sighed in defeat and forced herself to admit that the only reason she was sitting here having dinner with James was because she wanted it for herself. Selfishly, needfully, desperately for herself. In spite of all the things she could name that were wrong with James Nash, something about him made her feel so exquisitely right.

Why? She had no idea. She'd known him for less than half a day. According to her colleagues on the festival committee—especially Mayor March, who seemed to be one of his biggest fans—he was a celebrity, a playboy, a hedonist and a cad, not to mention a tourist, and he was never serious for a minute. Regardless of the giddy way he made Kirby feel, there was absolutely no future in anything that might be sparking between the two of them.

His life experiences could overflow every ocean on the planet, while hers would scarcely fill a juice glass. Who did she think she was, being turned on by a man like him?

But turned on she was, nonetheless.

And when she got right down to it, she understood why. He might be an icon of popular American culture, but he was also a man—just a man. As long as she kept her wits about her and stayed on her guard, there was no reason to think things would go too far between them. She could enjoy dinner with him, chat amiably, then invite him to be grand marshal of the Parallax Parade. If he said no, then she could thank him for a nice evening, leave with her dignity fully intact and never have to face him again.

And if he said yes, and she found herself shepherding him around town to a variety of festival functions, prolonging their contact for interminable hours, throwing them into close quarters over and over and over again...

Well, she could handle him, she told herself with less confidence that she would have liked to feel. He was just a man, she reminded herself again. Just a man, just a man, just a really incredible-looking, vastly charming, way too sexy, totally irresistible man. That was all.

Kirby bit back a groan and reached for her wine, completely forgetting that she didn't drink. Filling her mouth with the sweet, cool liquid, she swallowed a huge gulp without even giving herself a chance to savor it. Then, when she saw the heated way James was eyeing her from the other side of the table, she impulsively inhaled another gulp. And another. And another. And another. When she finally lowered her—wow, it was empty already?—glass, it was to find James still gazing at her over the rim of his own, a secret little smile playing about his lips.

"Like the wine?" he asked before enjoying an idle sip.

She nodded. "I don't usually imbibe, but this is really very good."

He settled his glass on the table and leaned forward. "If you don't usually imbibe, why did you steal my magnum of Perrier-Jouët this afternoon?"

She colored at that. "I, uh... I just, um... It was only because, er..." She cleared her throat with some difficulty. "Because the, uh...the bottle was so pretty?"

He grinned devilishly. "Never mind. Consider it a gift. But don't forget—it's always nice to share."

Instead of replying to his offer, she dropped her gaze silently to the table, tracing a finger leisurely around one of the roses in the linen cloth covering it.

"Now, then," James began again. "About that really, really, really big favor you needed to ask me."

Without looking up, Kirby told him, "It's not all *that* big a favor."

"No matter. You want me to do something that will make you feel indebted to me. That's all I need to know. What is it?"

When she glanced up, she found him looking way too eager for her comfort. Somehow, she knew that even if she asked him to dance the hokey-pokey naked with a duck on his head, in the middle of the town square, he'd do it, just to have her owing him an action of equal or lesser value in return.

"I, um...I mean, *we*...the committee...the Welcome Back, Bob Comet Festival committee," she clarified hastily, "would like to extend an invitation to you. Actually," she added, hoping she wasn't pouring it on too thick, "it's more like the whole town of Endicott would like to extend an invitation to you."

James grinned as he twirled his wineglass lazily by its stem. A languid, yet highly erotic, fire was burning in his eyes. "The whole town, huh? Oh, goody. The stakes on this favor just keep getting higher and higher, don't they?"

Kirby ignored his comment, and instead plunged ahead. "We, uh...the committee, I mean...we seem to have lost the grand marshal of the Parallax Parade, and—"

"You lost him?" James interrupted. "How could you lose a grand marshal?"

"It wasn't our fault," she assured him. "Rufus—"

"Rufus?"

"—just got a better offer, that's all."

"Rufus?" James repeated. "Are there actually people still alive today named Rufus?"

"Rufus Laidlaw," she specified. She gave her forehead a mental smack when she realized the distinction would be completely meaningless to James, unless he happened to be a big fan of laxative commercials. "He's an actor. A local boy who went west and became a big star and—"

"I don't know any big stars named Rufus Laidlaw," James interjected. "And believe me, I know *a lot* of stars. Don't forget Ashley Evanston."

Kirby's roundabout invitation ceased completely at that. "I thought you said you *didn't* know Ashley Evanston."

"Well, not in the Biblical sense, but I do know her. And lots of others, too. Though you'd never catch me dropping names," he added parenthetically. "That's so gauche, don't you think?"

Frankly, Kirby didn't know what to think. The conversation had taken a turn she'd never meant to steer them into. "I...I guess so."

"On the other hand, however," James continued, "I don't know a single person in Hollywood named Rufus."

"Rufus Laidlaw is, uh...he's kind of up-and-coming," Kirby said, trying not to squirm in her chair.

"What's he done?"

She dropped her gaze and went back to tracing the rose in the tablecloth. "Most recently?" she stalled.

"Or ever."

"He, uh...actually, he launched his career as a dancing can of corn in a commercial for the Indiana Corn Growers Association."

When James said nothing in response, Kirby glanced up to find him studying her with an expression that suggested he didn't know whether she was being serious or not.

"But he's appeared nationally in a laxative commercial." She rushed on to Rufus's defense. She had, after all, gone to school with Penelope Laidlaw and knew Rufus by default. She felt like she owed him *something.*

"I see," James murmured.

"And...and he's just received this great offer, for an even bigger part, which is why he can't be the grand marshal of the parade after all. Kellogg's has hired him to be their national spokesflake for a new breakfast cereal."

"National spokesflake," James repeated.

Kirby nodded, avoided his gaze and went back to her original point. Unfortunately, because she was so addled by the way James was gazing at her—as if she were a generous slice of cheesecake and he was more than ready for dessert—the single, simple question became a long, drawn-out storytelling event, all spoken in the inquisitive tense.

"Anyway?" she began. "With Rufus bailing out on us to become a national spokesflake? Now we need someone else to be the grand marshal of the Parallax Parade? And although we'd like for the grand marshal to be someone local? There really aren't any other local celebrities besides Rufus? Well, except for Dierdre Mahoney? Who was the Indiana Corn Queen one year? But she's already been a grand marshal of the Christmas Parade? Three times? And, anyway? What we were wondering? Was if you might be interested in taking Rufus's place?"

James studied Kirby from the other side of the table, scarcely hearing a word she said. He was too busy noting how the yellow candlelight gilded her hair and skin, how her blue eyes seemed to grow darker every time she looked at him, how the gauzy white fabric of her dress nestled against a perfect half circle of ivory skin above. He was too caught up in the faint scent of lavender that surrounded her, and in the way the wine had dampened her lips and pinked her cheeks.

And he was wondering how she was going to taste, how she was going to feel, how she was going to sound when he made love to her. Because at that moment, he knew without question that before his sojourn in Endicott was over, he'd be making love to Kirby.

Too, he was pondering what her reaction would be if he attempted it right then, if he simply stood abruptly and swept the dishes off the table with one savage gesture, tugged her out of her chair, pushed up her skirt and pulled down her panties, and made love to her right there amid the remnants of their repast.

And he decided very quickly that she was much too far away. "I'm sorry," he said when she seemed to have stopped speaking. "What did you say? I was thinking about something else."

"I, uh," she began. She took a moment to visibly muster her courage, then tried again. "On behalf of the Welcome Back, Bob Comet Festival committee and the citizens of Endicott, Indiana, I'd like to extend an invitation to you to be grand marshal of the Parallax Parade this year."

James studied her warily. She was obviously out of her mind if she thought he would agree to such a thing. He was a man who tried his damnedest to *avoid* public exposure, and even at that, he too frequently found himself decorating the covers of tabloids, providing sound bites for celebrity bushwhacker TV shows and other such rot. Yet here she was asking him to sit up on top of a big papier-mâché float, waving the crowds to just come and get him.

Not bloody likely.

In spite of his conviction, however, he heard himself asking, "Just what would being grand marshal of the Parallax Parade involve?"

Instead of being delighted that he might actually consider the invitation, Kirby appeared to deflate some at his interest. After a seemingly heartfelt sigh of discontent, she frowned and said, "Oh, not that much. You'd just be the centerpiece of the entire festival is all."

James didn't like the sound of that. "Oh, gee, is that all?" he asked dryly.

She nodded disconsolately, which he considered odd since she still seemed to think he was going to accept. Then she told him, "You'd have to show up at all the festival functions, and—"

"What kind of festival functions?"

She shrugged. "Well, the Parallax Parade is the first one—it will officially launch the festival this Sunday. In addition to that, the major events are the Comet Stomp Dance, the Parsec Picnic in the Park, the Castor and Pollux Two-Legged Race, the Triton

Tug-O-War, the Milky Way Marathon and the Regolith Regatta. Those are the biggies.''

James continued to twirl his wineglass by its stem, watching the pale gold liquid sheet on the sides, amazed to find himself actually considering her proposal. There was no way he could do it, he immediately told himself. He'd come to Endicott to consort with Bob, to study the comet from a stargazer's point of view and to enjoy a few quiet weeks by himself after an endless summer of partying.

If he consented to her request, he'd be surrounded by people, eaten alive by the media and the masses, and when the feeding frenzy was over, there would be nothing of himself left for himself to enjoy. Such was the price he paid for living the life he led. He had no privacy, kept no secrets, claimed no trustworthy friends, called no place home. And everyone on the planet— *everyone*—thought they owned him, body and soul.

In spite of that, James had hoped to maintain a relatively low profile while he was in Endicott. He'd told no one where he was going, and had come to town only to get as up close and personal as he could with the comet, because he'd been fascinated by comets since he was a boy old enough to read about them. He'd intended to spend virtually every moment of the three weeks he'd be in town right in his hotel suite, parked behind his telescope.

Then, his first day in town, he'd leveled his telescope not on a comet, but on an entirely different kind of heavenly body, one of exquisite perfection that surpassed celestial beauty. And ever since sighting her, James just couldn't seem to break free of Kirby's orbit. She was like Venus, the evening star. Beautiful, ethereal, unattainable and hot enough to melt a man in a nanosecond. And he had become her unwitting satellite.

Now she was asking him to do something that was really quite unthinkable, something that would not only bite significantly into the time he'd allotted for his comet viewing, but something that would compromise his very existence for the next three weeks. Nevertheless, there was still one question spiraling around in his head that commanded consideration.

''And what's *your* role in the life of a grand marshal, Kirby?''

At his softly uttered question, that perfect half circle of ivory skin above the neckline of her dress was immediately stained pink with the heat of a blush. "I, uh..." she stammered. "My, um...my position with the committee is kind of related to, uh... hospitality."

"Hospitality," he repeated.

She nodded nervously but didn't elaborate.

James curled his fingers more tightly around the stem of his wineglass, but his gaze never left hers as he stated, "Define 'hospitality.'"

Again, she seemed unusually nervous about something, and he found himself wanting very badly to know what precisely that something might be.

"I, uh," she hedged again, "I'm sort of the PR person."

"Could you be a little more specific?"

"I'm kind of, um, responsible for making sure VIP visitors have everything they need."

He was beginning to like the sound of that. "VIPs?"

"Mmm-hmm."

He couldn't help but notice that her murmured response was a bit strangled. He smiled, going in for the kill. "Is there any VIP in specific on your list that you're to be responsible for?"

"Oh, I guess...yeah."

"And who would that VIP be?"

She eyed him quickly, then let her gaze ricochet around the room. "Specifically?"

"Specifically."

"Well, *specifically,* I'd, uh...sort of act as the grand marshal's, um...escort."

"An escort? Really? That sounds very intriguing. I mean, the word *escort* just conjures up all kinds of images, doesn't it? All kinds of connotations."

She dropped her gaze back down toward the table, and quickly clarified, "No, I mean I'd be your, um...escort to the different festival functions. Just to make sure you...have everything you...need."

Her voice was growing more dismal, her expression more crestfallen, with every word she spoke. James couldn't help but smile.

She was honestly bothered by the idea of being forced to accompany him to social functions.

How very extraordinary. There were scores of women out there who would duel to the death for such an opportunity. Not that James wanted anything to do with such desperate creatures, naturally. But a man did like to see at least a *little* enthusiasm in a potential date. Kirby seemed more willing to face the guillotine than the prospect of an evening by his side.

"Okay, I'll do it," he heard himself say suddenly, as surprised by the announcement as Kirby seemed to be.

"What?" she asked incredulously when she snapped her head back up to meet his gaze.

"I said I'll do it," he repeated.

"You can't be seri..." she began, clamping her teeth down over her lower lip and literally biting off her words before they were complete. "I mean—" She tried again. "I thought...that is...I've heard you're not the kind of person who would, um...uh..."

"Take advantage of an opportunity to spend more time with a beautiful, desirable woman who acts like she doesn't want any part of me, in spite of that come-hither look in her eyes whenever she sees me?" he supplied helpfully.

"Uh, no," she said with a bemused shake of her head, her cheeks reddening at his blatant admission. "Actually, I meant I've heard you're not the kind of person who would willingly seek the spotlight."

"Oh, *that*," he said with a smile. "Well, no, normally I don't. Not unless my reward for doing so is to spend time with a beautiful, desirable woman who acts like she doesn't want any part of me, in spite of that come-hither look in her eyes whenever she sees me."

"Oh."

He waited for her to say something more, but she only turned her head toward the window, to the view of Endicott as it lay bathed in the shimmering light of a late-setting sun. James, too, turned to enjoy the vista, and saw the entire town stained with orange and red and gold, giving him the impression that it was some kind of dormant El Dorado just waiting to be plundered of its treasure.

Of course, Endicott's most precious gem was already within his reach, he thought as he settled his gaze on Kirby again. He need only extend his arm the length of a table barely big enough for two to seize that most dazzling of jewels and hold her in the palm of his hand. For some reason, though, the last thing he wanted to do was seize her. Yes, he wanted Kirby. Badly. But somehow it didn't seem right to steal her away from this place.

In addition to that, women always gravitated toward James long before he even had a chance to approach them. Kirby, on the other hand, seemed to be magnetically repelled. And at the moment, the thought of actually *pursuing* a woman for a change was somehow oddly appealing.

"I would have thought you would be pleased by my acceptance of your offer," he told her. "After all, you did invite me."

She shook her head almost imperceptibly. "No, *I* didn't invite you. I only extended the invitation on behalf of—"

"The good people of Endicott—yes I know," James said irascibly. "I'd still think you would be pleased."

She dropped her gaze back to the tablecloth, her shoulders drooping. "It's not that."

"Then what?"

Abruptly she stood, and before he realized her intention, she quickly crossed the room and snatched her purse up from the table where she'd dropped it. Then she twisted the doorknob and jerked open the door, and James thought she meant to leave without even saying goodbye. But at last she seemed to recall that she was, in effect, an ambassador for the city of Endicott.

Glancing back over her shoulder, but not quite looking at him, she said hastily, "I'm so glad you've accepted our invitation to be grand marshal of the parade, Mr. Nash. I'll be in touch with you tomorrow morning with all the particulars." She took a step forward, then seemed to remember something else and turned back around. "Thank you for dinner."

Then she disappeared through the door, closing it soundlessly behind her. And all James could do was feel strangely melancholy about the fact that they'd never even had a chance to enjoy dessert.

Four

Four

"So what are you going to do about James Nash?"

Kirby stirred her coffee slowly and eyed Angie Ellison warily,
not sure how she should respond to her friend's question. Along
with Rosemary March, the three friends were winding up their
regular lunch with their regular coffee and their regular dessert.

Kirby's feelings at the moment, however, were anything but
regular. Their conversation today had been strange even when she
took into consideration the presence of Bob looming out there on
the cosmic horizon. Of course, barely twenty-four hours had
passed since her initial meeting with James Nash, so she could
hardly be responsible for feeling strange right now, but still...

Kirby didn't want to say anything to her friends—because she
wasn't sure what kind of reception she'd get from them—but it
sounded to her like that darned comet really was going to grant
their wishes.

Last night, Angie had broken into a man's house and had come
face-to-face with a mobster. A mobster! A really cute one, too,
evidently. What could possibly be more exciting than that? And
Rosemary's archrival from high school, Willis Random, had re-

turned to town to study the comet, and was living right under Rosemary's roof. If that wasn't an opportunity just rife with revenge potential, Kirby didn't know what was.

Why should Angie and Rosemary get their wishes, and not her? A forever-after kind of love had seemed the most likely of their wishes to come true, yet it was nowhere near within her grasp. The only man she'd met lately was James Nash. If that was Bob's idea of a joke, well... She could do very nicely without that kind of intergalactic humor, thank you very much. James Nash wasn't capable of *any* kind of love, let alone the forever-after variety. Who did Bob think he was kidding?

Darned comet.

"Kirby?"

Rosemary's quietly uttered inquiry brought her attention back to the conversation at hand. "What?" she asked morosely.

"What are you going to do about James Nash?" She echoed Angie's earlier question.

Kirby shifted her gaze from one woman to the other. "I'm going to stay as far away from that promiscuous playboy Peeping Tom as I can. What else?"

"That's going to be kind of tough," Angie pointed out, "with him being the grand marshal and you being the grand marshal's handler."

Kirby swallowed hard. She didn't even want to think about "handling" James Nash. "Don't worry about it," she assured her friends. "I can be his caretaker from a distance. He doesn't like to go out in public anyway."

"If that's the case, then why did he agree to be grand marshal?" Rosemary asked.

Kirby was still trying to figure that one out. "I have no idea," she said honestly.

Rosemary wiggled her eyebrows playfully. "From what you've told us so far, it doesn't sound to me like he wants to be kept at a distance. Sounds to me like he wants to stay very close to you."

Kirby shook her head. "Only because he won't accept the fact that I'm in no way interested in him. The concept of himself as an undesirable mate doesn't seem to quite gel in that egocentric brain of his."

"Or maybe it's because he's seen you naked," Angie added oh-so-helpfully, with a mischievous little smile. "And hey, Kirby, the best part is…you didn't even have to *try*."

She blushed again. Every time Angie or Rosemary had brought up the subject of James having seen her naked—and they'd brought up the subject over and over and *over* again—Kirby had felt her face flame. And not with embarrassment, either, which is what she told herself any self-respecting woman with a spotless reputation would do.

No, the heat that wound through her lately seemed to be coming from a far more libidinous source than embarrassment. For some reason, the knowledge that James had seen her au naturel sent a shiver of something she'd never felt before shuddering through her body. For the life of her, Kirby couldn't begin to identify what it was. She only knew that the concept of nudity seemed to be taking up an inordinate amount of space in her brain lately.

And not just her own nudity, either. Now every time someone mentioned that James Nash had seen her naked, it made Kirby want to see him naked, too. After all, it seemed only fair.

She forced her attention reluctantly back to the conversation at hand. "No, I think it's just because the guy has never met a woman who didn't want to jump right into bed with him immediately upon realizing who he is. I'm an aberration to him."

Rosemary made a face. "Kirby, you're a thirty-year-old virgin. You're an aberration to *everybody*."

Kirby started to object on her own behalf when Angie did it for her. Sort of. "Hey, Rosemary, it's not like she hasn't *tried*," her supposed friend pointed out—yet again. "Give her *some* credit."

Kirby gaped at both of them. "Thanks a lot, you guys. You make it sound like I'm clubbing every single man in town over the head and dragging him back to my cave."

Rosemary and Angie exchanged knowing looks, then both nervously dropped their gazes to the table and began to fiddle with their silverware. A lot.

Kirby gaped again. "I have *not* been doing that."

"Well, no, not literally," Angie said, still avoiding Kirby's gaze.

"Or figuratively, either," Kirby insisted.

Rosemary, at least, looked up when she spoke. "Well, there was that little episode with Henry Monroe last year."

Kirby was the one to glance away this time as she recalled the incident, one the gossip mill had obviously delighted in spreading around. There was nothing to it, of course, just a little misunderstanding with the man in question. Still, she knew she sounded a little anxious when she responded, "Oh, please, that was a complete accident. I wasn't trying to...to...to..."

"To lure him into your bed and have your way with him?" Angie asked helpfully.

"Of course not!" Kirby insisted.

"What about that little, uh, mishap with Mark Benedict a few months ago?" Rosemary added. "Was that an accident, too? You were *almost* naked that time."

"Of course it was an accident!" Kirby assured them, still averting her gaze, wanting to forget that episode as badly as she did the Henry Monroe one. "What else could it have been but an accident?"

She cringed when Angie said, "An attempt to lure him into your bed to have your way with him?"

"It's all gossip," she insisted. "All of it. I've never tried to...to...to..."

"To lure men into your bed and have your way with them?" Angie asked again. "Because that's the way it's been sounding for the last couple of years, Kirb. Like you've been trying hard as all get-out to offer up your virginity to the first interested taker."

Rosemary nodded avidly in agreement. "Yeah. Except that there haven't been any interested takers, because no man in town wants to deflower the local virgin, because she's just too damn nice for something like that."

"But please, Kirby," Angie added quickly, "by all means, correct us if we're wrong."

Kirby took a deep breath and held it, counting to ten. When

she finally opened her mouth to hotly defend herself further, Angie started up again and cut her off.

"You know, Kirb, this James Nash thing could be a blessing in disguise."

Kirby narrowed her eyes at her friend. "What are you talking about?"

Angie's shrug was about as nonchalant as a wooden stake through the heart would be. "Just that...you know. You and he could benefit mutually from, uh...working together."

Kirby tilted her head to the other side and squinted at her friend some more. "I still don't follow you."

But Rosemary evidently did, because she piped up, "Ooh, Angie, that is *such* a good idea. It would be perfect."

But Kirby was still at a loss. "What's a good idea? What would be perfect?"

Known for neither her discretion nor her tact, Angie stated bluntly, "James could pop your cherry for you."

"*What?*" Kirby asked incredulously.

"Think about it, Kirby," Rosemary interjected. "You obviously want to lose your virginity, James Nash obviously wants to, um...have a good time while he's in town. He doesn't know of your untouched status—not that he would probably care anyway, if what the tabloids say is true—so it wouldn't be a, uh...deterrent to him. So to speak. It's the perfect solution for both of you."

"It is *not* perfect," Kirby said indignantly. "There's been more to my motivation the last few years than just losing my virginity. A lot more."

"So then you admit that you've been trying your damnedest to lose it," Angie said with a laugh.

Rosemary joined in the levity. "Especially if you've been targeting guys like Henry Monroe and Mark Benedict."

"I have *not*—"

"Oh, come on, Kirby," Angie said with another chuckle. "Give it up. You can't fool us. We've known you too long."

Kirby fairly growled at her friends. "Okay," she conceded. "I admit that for the last few years I've been, uh...altering my standards a little where my, um...sexual identity is concerned."

Angie's smile broadened. "You're tired of being the town virgin, so you've been looking for a cherry popper."

"I'm tired of being alone, so I've been looking for Mr. Right," Kirby corrected her friend.

"Whatever you want to call him, he still holds the same basic function." Angie leaned back in her chair and crossed her arms over her midsection, grinning with satisfaction.

"It's just that...that Mr. Right doesn't seem to exist in Endicott right now," Kirby continued, feeling the frustration that had dogged her for years rising to the fore. "All of the good ones are taken, and the ones that are left are looking for something that I don't have. Namely, um...experience."

She leaned forward and propped her elbows on the table, expelling a restless breath as she tried to bite back the bitterness that threatened to join the frustration. Then, unable to stop herself, she continued. "I mean, there was a time when a woman's virtue was considered a prize, you know? But not these days—*noooo*. These days, any woman who saves it for someone special is considered a sexual dysfunction just waiting to happen. It's the old catch-22—no one wants a virgin, but how's a virgin going to lose it if no one wants her?"

Angie and Rosemary exchanged glances again. "*That's* the old catch-22?" Rosemary asked. "I thought the old catch-22 was something totally different."

Kirby ignored her and continued with what had become a really good righteous indignation. "I mean, what kind of man would turn that down, you know? What's so wrong with saving it for someone you love? Why is it so horrible to wait? Because frankly, I'm not sure how much longer I *can* wait. I hate the waiting. The waiting is driving me crazy. Crazy. If I have to wait much longer I'm going to...to...to..." She drove both hands impatiently through her hair. "I'll go positively...absolutely...completely...utterly..."

"Wow," Rosemary interjected. "Talk about your woman nearing her sexual peak."

Angie nodded. "And nobody there to help her enjoy it. Kirby, honey," she added hastily, "you gotta do something about this quick. Otherwise, you'll just lose it."

"Don't you *see?*" Kirby shouted out suddenly, all vestige of self-control having deserted her. "That's exactly what I've been trying to do! Lose it! But nobody wants to take it from me!"

Then, when she realized what she had just confessed at close to a billion decibels, when she saw that every single person in the Maple Leaf Café had turned their attention to her outraged outburst, she dropped her head into her hands and shook with humiliation.

"Like I said," Angie began again, her voice softer now, more understanding, "this situation with James Nash could turn out to be just the thing you need."

When Kirby awoke before sunrise the following morning, she remained in bed with her eyes closed for a good fifteen minutes, trying to convince herself that she had, in fact, been fast asleep during all those terrible things that had been happening to her for the past couple of days. Surely they were just horrible, horrible nightmares, and not a cruel reality to which she had suddenly become subjected.

Unfortunately, when she finally opened her eyes, she was forced to admit that the past two days really had happened. James Nash had not been a figment of her sexually repressed and romantically overwrought imagination. He really was in Endicott. He really had agreed to be the grand marshal of the Parallax Parade. And Angie and Rosemary really had tried to convince her that letting him pop the cherry she was so insistent on preserving, as Angie had so maddeningly kept putting it, would be the best thing for her social life in Endicott.

And once Kirby had revealed to them that James had in fact tried to seduce her in the library, they really had, as one, urged her to go for it.

Then again, that seduction attempt was a piece of reality that was still a bit fuzzy, she had to admit. She was, after all, not particularly well versed in that whole man/woman courtship/seduction thing, and maybe what she had thought was a seduction attempt had actually been nothing more than some kind of "guy" ritual that men engaged in just prior to asking a woman to have dinner with them. Like that little hopping motion peacocks danced when happening upon a likely peahen, or the expulsion of that pink dewlap thingy that male chameleons used with such success when wooing female chameleons.

Then again, she thought further, male animals generally just sort of pounced on the unsuspecting females after all the hopping and the dewlap, whether the females in question liked it or not. Didn't they? Hmm...

Kirby made a mental note to ask Angie and Rosemary all about that the next time she saw them. Then again, did she honestly trust their advice? After all, their suggestion that losing her virginity to James Nash, who, granted, was the *only* likely candidate for such a thing, would make her a more marketable commodity among the single men in Endicott was just too preposterous to consider.

Wasn't it?

Of course it was.

She chased the thought from her brain and forced herself from bed, then stumbled toward the kitchen to fire up the coffeemaker. With the warm aroma of fresh coffee fortifying her a bit, she made her way to the front door to collect the morning edition of the *Endicott Examiner* from her porch. Unfortunately, it looked as though Seth, the thirteen-year-old delinquent who delivered her daily dose of news, had missed the front porch entirely. Again. Because there was no sign of the newspaper anywhere.

Kirby glanced both left and right, heedful of the fact that she was still dressed in the white cotton baby-doll nightie that the warm September nights commanded. But the sun had barely smudged the morning sky with bits of lavender and orange and pink. Except for the finches and robins and cardinals serenading her, the neighborhood was empty. So, unconcerned, she stepped barefoot out onto the porch and began a surreptitious search of her shrubs.

To no avail. Emboldened by the solitude surrounding her, Kirby moved down the front stairs to the slightly curving walkway that led to her drive. Nothing. She stepped back into the cool, dewy grass and eyed the roof, where Seth had been known to deposit her paper when he was feeling particularly surly. Nothing. Nothing in the azaleas, nothing in the black-eyed Susans, nothing in the mums. Farther and farther from her front door Kirby wandered in search of her newspaper, but she never even found a headline.

Not until someone cleared his throat and called out, "Looking for this?"

Which was when Kirby spun around to find James Nash seated in the white wicker swing at the other end of her wraparound porch. She hadn't noticed him before because her front door opened onto the other leg of the L-shaped veranda, and naturally he wasn't enough of a gentleman to have made his presence immediately known.

But there he was all the same, sitting quite comfortably on the flowered chintz cushion, reading her newspaper by the light of the yellow bug lamp behind him. And drinking what appeared to be a mimosa, if the crystal flute sitting on the porch near his feet was any indication.

Kirby dropped her hands to her hips and said, "What are you doing here?"

James folded the newspaper and set it aside before answering, "What has suddenly become my life's work. Waiting for you."

"Why?"

He smiled, slowly, lasciviously, and only then did she realize that his gaze was lingering not on her face, but lower. Like right about…thigh height. Kirby colored when she remembered what she was—barely—wearing. Would there ever come a time when she could actually have a conversation with this man without blushing like a virgin?

Well, no, she supposed not. Not as long as she was what she was. Namely, a blushing virgin.

"Why?" he echoed. "Because I thought maybe I could have you for breakfast."

"Don't you mean you thought maybe you could *join* me for breakfast?"

He shook his head slowly, his gaze still fixed on her legs. "No."

"I see."

"Me, too. More than I anticipated. Why don't you invite me in?"

"Why don't you hand over my newspaper?"

He scooped up the other sections of the neglected paper and began to shuffle them back together. "You might want to be careful what you wear when you leave your home in the morning," he cautioned her blandly with another, not-so-bland perusal of her bare legs. "According to the newspaper, there's a crime wave sweeping your community."

Kirby couldn't help but chuckle. "Crime? Here? You're joking, right? The last crime I heard about in Endicott was when Fuzzy Fowler and Hugo Klosterman got caught tipping Mrs. Irwin's cows three years ago."

James held up the local section of the paper and pointed to a tiny article in the lower right-hand corner. "Well, this puts that heinous cow tipping to shame. It says here that the Philadelphia mob is moving in on a local pharmaceutical company."

Kirby waved a hand airily without concern. "Oh, that."

James arched his dark eyebrows in surprise. "'Oh, that'? That's all you have to say?"

"It's not as bad as it sounds," she assured him. "Angie's on the case."

"Angie?"

"My friend, Angie Ellison. She's the one who wrote the article for the paper."

He nodded as he seemed to be recalling something. "That would be the friend you identified the other day as being the most gullible woman in America?" he asked.

"That's the one."

"She's on the case, is she?"

"You got it."

"Now why does that make me feel not one iota better?"

James went back to folding up the newspaper, blindly, because he continued to ogle Kirby without inhibition as he did so. And although she told herself she should be hot with anger at the blatancy of his study, she found herself growing warm inside for entirely different reasons.

He looked wonderful. His black hair fell unfettered to just past his shoulders, like black satin. Black, too, were his clothes—a collarless, short-sleeved shirt left open at the throat, which somehow made his bronzed skin appear even darker, and baggy trousers. Yet for some reason, instead of making him appear forbidding, the color suited him. It was dramatic, chic and powerful.

And, she forced herself to admit, utterly opposite herself in every way imaginable. Nope. Regardless of Angie's and Rosemary's assurances to the contrary, James Nash was in no way the right candidate for her, uh...deflowering. Still, that didn't mean she couldn't at least be civil to him. He was the grand marshal, after all.

"I suppose you're expecting me to invite you in for breakfast, aren't you?" she asked.

"Of course I am. I'm sorry, I thought I made that clear." He rose from the swing, then bent to retrieve his drink, in one swallow consuming what was left.

"Where did that come from?" Kirby asked as she lifted her chin toward the now-empty champagne flute, sidestepping temporarily the question of whether or not he would be welcome to join her for breakfast.

"There's a wet bar in the car," he told her in a matter-of-fact voice, as if he thought everyone kept a wet bar in their back seat, just in case they might want to have a mimosa while they perused a stranger's morning newspaper and/or invaded a person's front porch.

Kirby shifted her gaze over her shoulder, scanning her street first to the left and then to the right. "And, um...where exactly is your car?"

He shrugged as he took a few steps forward. His shoes scraped slightly over the cement of her front porch as he approached, their leisurely rhythm completely at odds with the rapid, erratic pounding of her heart.

"I told Omar to take the morning off," he said softly. He didn't stop moving until he stood at the rail looking down at her, the position giving him the impression of even more height, even more authority, even more power.

Just what she needed, she thought as another wave of shimmering heat washed over her. "So I guess that means you're stranded here, right?"

He dropped his mouth open and smacked his forehead in what

was obviously phony self-deprecation. "Oh, man, I didn't even think about that. By giving my driver the morning off, I've stranded myself here at your house with you, haven't I? Gee, *now* what am I going to do?"

Kirby shook her head, not so much at James, but at the parade of lascivious ideas she was suddenly entertaining in response to his question. Personally, she could think of quite a few things for him to do, all of them pretty racy, all of them involving herself and none of them in any way appropriate for her to be considering in her pajamas.

"I don't know," she lied. "But if you'll hand over my newspaper, *I'm* going to go inside *my* house and fix *myself* some Belgian waffles." She extended her hand toward him, palm up, a silent indication that he should hand over her morning news. Now.

"Would you...care for a little company?" he asked.

The question was evidently nothing more than a formality, because instead of handing over her newspaper, he folded it in half and tucked it under his arm, then made his way to her front door. Obviously, he thought she was going to welcome him into her home. Obviously, he fully expected her to include him in her daily routine. Obviously, he was of the opinion that she would gladly invite him to have breakfast with her.

Obviously, he was right. Darn it.

Kirby expelled a helpless sound and ran her fingers hastily through her hair, hesitating before following him into her own house. This was ridiculous. She'd known the man only a matter of days, but already she'd shared more with him than with any other man she'd ever known. Dinner. Morning pleasantries. Decorating tips. And lest she forget—which of course, she would not—that soft, hopelessly stimulating touch in the library. He'd even seen her naked. The whole situation was just too bizarre.

"Kirby?"

When she heard the summons, she glanced up to find him standing at her open front door, extending his hand toward the interior, as if he were the one who lived there and had issued the invitation to breakfast.

Surrendering, both to James and to her own increasingly confusing thoughts, Kirby shuffled forward. As she passed him, she couldn't help but inhale deeply, drinking in the scent of him, savoring it as if she'd been denied the pleasure of fresh air for far too long. He smelled as good as he looked—a mixture of heat and spice and man. The combination almost overwhelmed her, so potent and unfamiliar to her was it.

"I, uh…" she began once she'd cleared the door and Nash, "I'll just go get dressed first, okay?"

"Oh, don't do that," he told her mildly. "Not on my account. You look just fine to me."

"Yes…well…considering your reputation, that's not exactly surprising."

Maybe his reaction wasn't surprising to her, James thought, but it was a hell of a surprise to him. Not the part about thinking she looked fine, of course. She was a beautiful woman, after all. She could be dressed like a water buffalo and he'd still be turned on at the sight of her. No, what came as such a surprise was the fact that he hadn't been able to turn himself *off* since he'd first sighted her through the lens of his telescope. That part was more than a little unusual.

It was no secret to anyone, least of all James, that he fell in and out of love at a rather rapid rate. And although it didn't happen often, when a woman wasn't interested in him, he took the hint and moved on to the next available comer. That wasn't because he was shallow, nor was it because he was unfeeling. It was simply the way his relationships ran. That was the nature of the dating game in his social circle.

But Kirby Connaught defied that nature. Because in spite of her assurances that she wasn't interested in starting anything with him, she hadn't been out of his thoughts once since he'd encountered her. Even while he slept, she danced through his head like a sugar plum fairy just begging to be nibbled.

And now here she was, within arm's reach of him, and all he could do was feel helpless. Because yet another unnatural phenomenon had overcome him. For some reason, where Kirby was concerned, James didn't quite feel certain of himself, and he was honestly at a loss for words.

So where his mind screamed at him to reach out for her, to

draw her into his arms and cover her mouth with his, to skim u. tantalizing little scrap of nightie from her shoulders and lead her back to her bedroom, back to the bed that was doubtless still warm from her body, still redolent of the fresh, clean, sweet scent of her...

He let his thoughts trail off and inhaled deeply, savoring her distinctive fragrance. Instead of doing all those things his mind commanded him to do, he only smiled and said, "I'll wait for you while you get dressed. Then maybe we can discuss at length my requirements as your grand marshal."

Her responding smile was one of clear relief that he was backing down, and he marveled again at her unwillingness to play the mating game with him.

"Help yourself to coffee," she said as she departed. "I won't be long."

As he wandered toward the kitchen, James absorbed his surroundings, having never been inside a pink stucco house before. *Simple, clean.* Those were the words she had used to describe her preferred surroundings the day he'd met her. And her house— like the woman herself—reflected that nicely.

The pale gold walls of the living room evolved into a butter yellow in the dining room and kitchen, while the plums and scarlets of the living room furniture blended well with the lavenders and roses of the kitchen and dining accents. The windows—and there were plenty of them—were covered by gauzy, ivory sheers, and the hardwood floors shone with the color of light refracted through honey. The walls were decorated with Art Deco prints of Miami hotels and eateries, which picked up the colors in the rooms. Bright pottery added splashes of additional shades of purple and red from atop the china cabinet, the cupboards and table centerpieces.

The effect on the whole was...calming. Warm. Subtle. Again, much like the woman herself. James liked the way Kirby decorated, the way she chose only a few colors and multiplied them tenfold by lightening and darkening them. It gave the impression of someone who was full of surprises. You think you know a color, when...*wham.* Suddenly you see it in a way you never thought it could be.

And he couldn't help wondering how much Kirby would charge to revamp, oh...say three houses, a ski cabin, a lakefront lodge, a beach house and four condos.

Ultimately he didn't have to wait long for her return. And when she did, she was wearing another shapeless, loose-fitting dress, this one made of a flowing fabric that was splashed with a million flowers. The hem fell below her knees and the sleeves well past her elbows, the wide, white collar bound above a long row of buttons with a big, and rather annoying, pink satin bow. Having accessorized the dress with sheer white stockings and pink Mary Janes, Kirby could have been the poster child for extended innocence. He sighed with heartfelt disappointment.

"Waffles okay for breakfast?" she asked as she breezed past him on a wave of lavender-scented air, oblivious to his blighted hope.

"I'd rather have you," he murmured.

She spun around at the comment, anger flashing in her eyes. "Okay, that does it," she said through bared teeth.

"What does it?" he asked, honestly mystified by her reaction. "What'd I do?"

But instead of answering outright, she only continued to glare at him as she said, "Since we're going to be forced to spend a lot of time together—"

"*Forced to,*" he echoed indignantly. "Speak for yourself."

"—then maybe it would be best if we just set down some ground rules right now," she continued as if he hadn't interrupted her.

This time James was the one to be wary. "What kind of ground rules?"

She inhaled a little shakily, then dropped her gaze to the floor and crossed her arms defensively over her midsection. James frowned. He spoke body language fluently, and he didn't like what Kirby was telling him.

"Rule number one," she began, "is that the reason I'm going to be spending time with you is *not* because I want to get to know you better in any kind of, um, *social* way. It's because it's my job."

Her soft, uncertain tone of voice, James noted, seemed to belie her confident announcement. But he said nothing to challenge her. Yet.

"My position on the festival committee," she continued, still speaking to the floor, "dictates that I be the person who makes sure the grand marshal, uh...has everything he needs. So I have no choice but to make myself available to you." She glanced up to meet his gaze levelly, then quickly clarified, "But I'll only be available in the strictest, most professional sense."

"Oh, come on, Kirby," he cajoled, "you know that's not the *only* reason you'll be spending time with me. You like me. You enjoy my company. Admit it."

"Rule number two—" she rushed on, acting as if she hadn't heard him, in spite of the pink in her cheeks that indicated she had "—because I'm with you in nothing but a professional capacity, I'm going to expect professional behavior—on both our parts."

James bit the inside of his jaw to contain the comment he felt trying to get out, about their respective parts—in this case, body parts—not necessarily being fully under their control. Therefore, he couldn't possibly guarantee, speaking for his own parts anyway, professional behavior.

When he said nothing in reply, Kirby shifted her gaze from his face to some vague point over his right shoulder. Between that and her expression of complete insecurity, James easily concluded that she was in no way committed to the little pep talk she was giving them both.

"Rule number three," she went on with obvious discomfort, "I'm not the kind of woman you're used to associating with, so you might as well just knock off all the sweet talk, because it's not going to work with me."

James opened his mouth, completely incapable of refraining from commenting on that, but she raised a hand, palm out, to halt him before he could say a word.

"I've lived in Endicott all my life," she told him. "I've never traveled far, I don't have overly sophisticated tastes and I really do believe that simple pleasures are the best. I'm a small-town girl in every sense of the word. And although I'm as interested in enjoying a romantic relationship as you appear to be—"

James heartened some at that, smiling at this sudden and unexpected turn of fortune.

"—you are in no way the kind of man I want to get involved with."

His smile fell.

"I'm not like the women you normally associate with," she repeated. "Trust me on this, and just let it go."

He eyed her skeptically. "You have two X chromosomes as opposed to one X and one Y, right?"

She eyed him suspiciously. "Uh, yeah..."

He smiled, obviously satisfied with her answer. "Well, then. You're just like the women I normally associate with," he concluded. "They're all female, too."

"And are they also all virgins?"

Kirby squeezed her eyes shut tight and gave herself a mental slap for blurting out her sexual status that way. How could she have revealed such a thing to a man like him? Not only was it none of his gosh-darned business, but she was certain it was in no way wise to speak of anything even remotely sexual in his presence. The man just exuded sex appeal as if he were a fountain of that very thing. *James Nash* and *sexual experience* were two redundant phrases. It would be downright dangerous to bring up the subject of sex with such a man. Why had she done such a thing?

Then again, Kirby thought further, maybe revealing her, uh...condition...would work to her advantage. Surely a man like him wouldn't be at all interested in someone as inexperienced as she was. He'd probably be terrified at the thought of having to initiate someone who had no idea what she was doing. No doubt, virgins were numero uno on the list of things to be avoided for men like him.

Unfortunately, when she opened her eyes, it was to find him gazing at her with much...interest. Uh-oh.

"So, it's true then," he said, the statement in no way inquisitive.

She wasn't sure she liked the sound of his voice. It positively reeked with fascination. "What's true?" she asked, although she was fairly certain she already knew what he was talking about.

No one in Endicott could ever keep a secret. James had probably been hanging around the Dew Drop Inn or Dot's Donut Hut, the two biggest information centers in town.

"It's true that you've never experienced..." His voice trailed off as he inhaled a long, thoughtful breath. "Sex," he finally finished frankly, his voice now lower, softer and smoother than she'd ever heard it. And she'd heard it pretty low, pretty soft and pretty smooth. "That no one has ever taken you to visit that incredible place that changes a person forever."

Kirby swallowed hard. "I, uh... No. I've never been there. I, um... Well, like I said. I haven't traveled far. Certainly not, um...to the, uh..." She cleared her throat with some difficulty and avoided his gaze. "Not there," she finally finished lamely.

James's smile grew broader. Uh-oh again.

"How very...extraordinary," he said.

Kirby wasn't altogether certain what to make of the comment, but she was pretty sure she should probably be concerned.

Before she could respond, however, James's expression grew speculative, and he said, "From what I hear, you're just dying to take a trip there, though, aren't you?"

She licked her suddenly dry lips, not wanting to lie, but not wanting to seem interested in his speculation, either. "I, ah...actually..."

"Because, you know, Kirby, I've been there *lots* of times myself. I'm *very* familiar with the territory." He met her gaze levelly, and she felt her temperature rise a hundred degrees. "I could show you all the most arousing sights, tip you to all the best places to eat...." His smile turned predatory. "I mean, they've practically given me a key to the city."

"I, ah..."

"You need but say the word, and you're as good as there. I guarantee you that I'd be an excellent—and very enthusiastic—tour guide."

"I...I...I...I think it might be better if I went with a different, um...tour guide the first time," she finally managed to tell him. "And I just haven't met the right man for that job is all."

"And why is that, I wonder?"

She lifted her chin a defensive fraction of an inch. "There aren't that many eligible bachelors in town."

"That's not what I heard," he immediately countered, altering his stance from suggestive to combative in less than a second.

So he really had been gossiping with the locals, she realized. Terrific. No telling how much he knew about her by now. Although she hated herself for revealing her worry, she found herself asking him, "And just what...exactly...*did* you hear?"

For the first time since returning to her kitchen, she saw James move. Instead of leaning insouciantly against the counter, sipping his coffee, which he'd been doing ever she'd come back into the room, he settled his mug down on the counter and straightened. Then, with a predatory gleam in his eyes that wreaked all sorts of havoc with her insides, he took a few steps forward.

And seeing as how hers was a pretty small kitchen, in no time at all James stood directly in front of her, gazing down at her with much interest—as if she were some kind of fascinating biological specimen he had just discovered under a microscope, and he couldn't wait to put her through all the tests.

"*I* heard that there are plenty of eligible bachelors in Endicott," he stated knowledgeably. "And I heard that you've made the acquaintance of just about *all* of them at one time or another." He paused, clearly for effect, before concluding. "*And* I heard that none of them has ever seen you naked—unlike me—but that that's *not* through any lack of trying on your part."

Kirby gaped at him, the heat of embarrassment winding from her head straight down to her toes. "I beg your pardon," she said, trying to fake as much indignation as she could.

James took one more step forward, something that brought him close enough that their bodies nearly—but not quite—touched. His heat surrounded her, overwhelmed her, as did his fragrance, his aura, his very being. And something inside Kirby responded to that nearness in the earthiest, most primitive manner possible. Suddenly, all she wanted to do was sway forward and loop her arms around his neck, pull his head down to hers, press her lips to his mouth and kiss the living daylights out of him.

His next words, however, halted her.

"In short, Miss Connaught," he began again, his voice a veritable purr now, "I've heard from some extremely good sources that you're not nearly as sweet and innocent as everyone in Endicott makes you out to be."

Five

Kirby's pulse rate quickened at his charge. Not sweet and innocent? Her? The last known living virgin of bedable age north of the Ohio River? Well, this was certainly news to her. If she wasn't so sweet and innocent, then how come she had so much trouble getting a date?

"I have no idea what you're talking about," she told him truthfully. "My reputation is spotless."

James nodded indulgently, but his smile turned knowing. "Oh, that part was never in question. Everyone has assured me that you are indeed as pure as Ivory soap and the proverbial driven snow. Although," he added, "in this day of acid rain and air pollution, that snow is a bit more soiled now than it was when that phrase was coined."

She opened her mouth to protest, but James cut her off, adding, "And as you'll recall, Ivory soap is only ninety-nine and forty-four one-hundredths percent pure. There's still that fifty-six one-hundredths to think about."

Kirby narrowed her eyes. "I reiterate—I have no idea what you're talking about."

"Let me put it this way. Yes, you are, as yet, unsampled by the men of this town—go figure. However," he added smugly, "you've been known on occasion to attempt—with rather dubious success—to *lure,* shall we say, the unsuspecting single men of Endicott into your parlor."

"Lure?" she repeated, striving for incredulous. "Me? I've never tried to *lure* anyone anywhere. I'm not sure I even know *how* to lure."

James eyed her blandly. "Oh, believe me, Kirby, you know how."

"I still don't understand—"

"Henry Monroe," he interrupted her easily.

Not that again. Not twice in two days. "Oh, please. Surely you don't believe that ridiculous story."

But he only rocked confidently back on his heels in response, assuring her that oh, yes, he did, too, believe that ridiculous story.

Kirby decided it would probably be pointless to deny that the episode had ever occurred, as much as she wished it hadn't. However, she could definitely elaborate on the gossips' version and make clear the truth of what had happened that evening nearly a year ago when Henry had come to her house.

"I suppose it's no secret," she conceded, "that I have tried, on occasion, in the past, to interest one or two men in Endicott. Not *lure*," she hastily emphasized. "Interest."

James's smile broadened even more. "I heard you've stopped just short of slipping them a Mickey and spinning a new suit for them in your web."

"That's not true," Kirby said adamantly. "Just because Henry Monroe sprained his ankle that one time—"

"Trying to escape your clutches."

"He was not trying to escape," she denied. "He only came over to fix my kitchen sink—"

"Which, from all reports, Mr. Monroe later claimed had absolutely nothing wrong with it."

"—and it was just by accident that my skirt got caught in his toolbox and sort of, um…got torn."

"More like it ripped right open," James charged. "Right down the front, too. Sounds kind of suspicious to me. Sounds like you were trying to, oh, say...tempt him to perform an altogether different kind of plumbing for you?''

Kirby's fingers curled involuntarily into fists. It had been an accident, she reminded herself. Okay, yes, she had invited Henry over in the hopes that the two of them might get something romantic off the ground. She had planned to have him look at her sink—which, regardless of what everyone said, really had been clogged—then she was going to thank him by fixing him a nice dinner afterward.

And okay, yes, she'd decided that if one thing had led to another afterward, and if the two of them had gotten a bit carried away by the romantic mood, well...she probably wouldn't have done much to protect her virginal reputation.

Unfortunately, at one point before dinner, she had bent to hand Henry a pipe wrench, only to have the toolbox slam shut on her skirt. And she hadn't realized it until she'd stood up, when her body had straightened easily, but the breezy chiffon of her skirt had not. Instead, that breezy chiffon had ripped completely down the middle, exposing considerably more flesh than Kirby had planned on exposing before dinner.

And Henry had been *so* shocked that sweet, innocent, Kirby Connaught, whom he'd always thought of as a dear, dear friend—really, like a little sister, for heaven's sake—would attempt to seduce him in such a blatant way, that he had, at the sight of her thighs, jumped up and fled her house, stumbling down the front steps as he went.

''It was an accident,'' Kirby assured James. ''It could have happened to anyone. And it was just an isolated incident.''

James nodded indulgently. ''Isolated incident, huh?''

''Isolated incident,'' she repeated.

''How about Mark Benedict?'' he asked. ''Was that an isolated incident, too?''

''Oh, now that *really* was an accident,'' Kirby insisted. ''He came over on the wrong day.''

''That's not what he says.''

''And just when did you speak to Mark Benedict, hmm?''

''The same time I spoke with Henry Monroe. This morning at

Dot's Donut Hut, when Omar and I stopped in for coffee on the way to your house.''

"Oh, well, see there?'' she demanded. "It's a conspiracy.'' Then, in an effort to deflect the conversation from her own romantic mishaps, she added, "And just what were you doing in Dot's Donut Hut, anyway, Mr. I-Can't-Possibly-Be-Seen-in-Public-Because-of-My-Adoring-but-Slightly-Homicidal-Fans?''

His posture changed suddenly at that. He dropped all his weight to one foot and lifted a finger in idle speculation. "You know,'' he said, distracted for a moment, "that's something else about this town. No one has mobbed me here.'' He sounded almost disappointed by the realization. "They've all recognized me, but no one has tried to trample me. Why is that?''

Kirby shrugged. "Maybe you're not as big a deal as you thought you were?''

He gaped at that. "I *beg* your pardon?''

"Or maybe we're just more polite here than in other places you frequent?''

He thought about that for a moment. "Yeah, well, true, Miss Manners would go bankrupt if she set up business here, but I don't think that's it, either.''

"Maybe it just takes more to impress us here than something like international celebrity.''

Now he was clearly incredulous. "What could possibly be more impressive than international celebrity?''

Kirby made a face at him. "Gee, I don't know. Good deeds. Acts of heroism. Selfless giving. Just a shot in the dark, mind you, but...''

He seemed to become wrapped up in thought for a moment, then shook his head, as if physically trying to clear it. "Dot's Donut Hut,'' he reiterated, bringing them back to the matter at hand. "The reason I didn't worry about my adoring public was because it was 4:00 a.m. and I didn't think the place would be occupied. Imagine my surprise to find a thriving business.''

"It's close to Industrial Park,'' Kirby told him. "And the third shift at the Peter Piper Pickle Plant has plenty of part-time people.''

James smiled. "Say that again—three times, real fast—and see what happens."

She ignored him.

So he continued on blithely. "Well, all I can say is that it was awfully funny how most of the men at the Donut Hut this morning seemed to be survivors of your seduction attempts. And they all went out of their way to warn me about you when they found out I was headed out this way."

"Oh, I just bet they did."

"Now, about the time you had Mark Benedict come over to fix a crack in your ceiling? I understand that you greeted him at the front door wearing nothing but a robe. A short, skimpy robe. One that was wet in some pretty significant places, because you were conveniently just stepping out of the shower when he arrived at the designated time."

"I *was* just stepping out of the shower," Kirby explained. "But I was expecting Angie and Rosemary, with whom I was going to a movie, not Mark. *He* was supposed to come on Thursday, not Wednesday."

James eyed her doubtfully. "Do you normally answer the front door, wearing nothing but a robe?" he asked.

She arched an eyebrow at him, a silent reminder of the day they had made their own acquaintance.

"Ah," he remarked when he recalled. "That's right. You do. Which really makes me wonder why you turned me down that day, since you're clearly so desperate to lose it."

"I am *not* desperate to 'lose it,'" she insisted. "There are just a few men in town I'd like to get to know better, that's all."

"And once you get to know them better," James surmised, "*then* you want to lose it, right?"

She felt herself coloring yet again. Until she met James Nash, she'd had no idea she had so many things to feel embarrassed about. "No," she said uneasily. "Not necessarily...."

But James only gazed at her in silence for a long time, as if he just couldn't for the life of him understand her. Finally, when she thought he would never speak again, he threw his arms out wide and demanded, "Why won't you try to lure me? Especially since I think I've made it perfectly clear that I am more than willing to be lured.''

Then he dropped his hands to his sides and bent forward until his face was within millimeters of her own. ''Just what is it, Kirby,'' he continued, ''that the Henry Monroes and Mark Benedicts of the world have that I don't have?''

She sighed heavily, wanting to contradict James's insistence that she was struggling so hard to lose her virginity, knowing instead that she could not. Because over the last couple of years, she really had gone out of her way to attract what few eligible, attractive men where left in Endicott. And she'd done it by throwing her virginity up onto the altar of sacrifice.

She'd been so certain that Bob would grant her wish by the time she was thirty. She'd been convinced that the comet wouldn't leave her high and dry, because the thing she had wished for fifteen years ago was so very noble, and so very simple.

Love. A forever-after kind of love. That was all Kirby had asked for. A nice man to care for her the way she would care for him, someone with whom she could build a home, a family, a life. And, truth be told, Bob or no Bob, she still hoped to find a man like that someday. Right here in her hometown. But how was that supposed to happen when all the men in her hometown refused to see her in anything but a sisterly, neighborly, daughterly light?

''What do they have that you don't have?'' she echoed James's question halfheartedly. ''An Endicott zip code, that's what.''

He cocked his head to one side, his black hair falling forward over his shoulder when he did so. For some reason, Kirby found herself wanting to reach out and touch the silky, ebony shafts, to let them fall and weave through her fingers, to wind them lightly around her hand and pull his head gently down to hers. But she checked herself just in time. Instead, she only watched him as he regarded her, and she wondered what he was thinking about.

''You told me over dinner the other night that the reason you came to Endicott was for the Bob Comet Festival,'' she said in an effort to thwart the silence that was fast overtaking them.

He nodded but still said nothing.

"Because you're a comet buff, I believe you said?"

Again, a silent nod in response.

"So you must be pretty familiar with Bob."

"Yes," he finally replied verbally. "I am."

"You know all about the local folklore? The legends? The myths?"

"I did my homework before I came to town."

"So then you know about the myth of the wishes."

Another nod. "Local citizens born in the year of the comet can supposedly make a wish upon Bob's next return, and that wish will be granted when Bob makes his third visit during their lifetime. Yes, I know all about it. I think the idea is rather quaint."

"It's also true."

She could see by his expression that he didn't for a moment believe her. "Is it?"

This time Kirby was the one to nod. "I was born in the year of the comet," she offered quietly.

She wondered why she was revealing all this to him, couldn't imagine what she hoped to gain by making someone like James Nash privy to her secret dreams and desires. Maybe she wanted to let him know how very important it was to her that she find a suitable man and settle down. Maybe once he realized that her one fervent wish in life was to be married with children, something he no doubt considered the kiss of death, he would leave her alone.

"I was fifteen the last time the comet came around," she began again.

James arched his eyebrows inquisitively as he considered Kirby in all her earnestness. Now this was a bit of local color he might enjoy learning more about. What would a woman like her have wished for when she was fifteen years old? he wondered. A new car? A date to the prom? An A on the algebra final? Clear skin? He tried to picture her as an adolescent, then quickly decided that she probably hadn't looked a whole lot different then than she did now.

"And did you make a wish the last time Bob paid a visit?" he asked her.

"Yes," she told him.

"What did you wish for?"

"I wished for true love," she stated without preamble. "The forever-after kind, the kind where two people commit to each other eternally with all their hearts, with all their souls, for richer, for poorer, in sickness and in health, 'til death do them part. The kind that ends up with a white picket fence and the pitter-patter of little feet."

James's reaction to her softly uttered revelation would have been the same if she had just told him a giant squid was sneaking up behind him. Shock, outrage, terror. Shock that a fifteen-year-old girl would already be planning her wedding, outrage that she had wasted a wish she could have used for something really good and terror that Bob was planning on granting her wish with James as the prize.

For a moment, he could only gape at her. When he finally did recover his voice, he asked incredulously, "You had one wish, and you wished to get married and have kids?"

She clearly couldn't understand his reaction, gaping back as she was at his charge. "Well, yeah."

"You wasted a perfectly good wish on something like that?"

"It wasn't a waste," she defended. "It was noble and heartfelt and—"

"Kirby, why did you wish for a husband and kids, something that you knew would happen anyway if you wanted it? Of course it was a wasted wish."

"How was I supposed to know it was going to happen anyway?" she demanded. "It *hasn't* happened anyway! Bob didn't grant my wish!"

"Yeah, because you insulted him by wishing for something like that."

She expelled an impatient little sound. "You are so ridiculous."

"*I'm* ridiculous?" he countered. "Hey, I'm not the one who wasted a perfectly good opportunity to wish for something really primo. You are."

"Oh, and what would you have wished for, Mr. Big Shot? Especially since you seem to get anything you want just by being James Nash, Most Desirable Man in America."

He said nothing for a moment, only settled his gaze on her face, studying her intently, feature by beautiful, delicate feature. Finally, very quietly, he told her, "I don't have quite everything I want."

"Wh-what more could you possibly w-want?" she asked him, tripping over the words as she uttered them.

Instead of answering her, James spun quickly around and returned to his original place by the counter. For some reason, he felt the need to put distance between them, but he didn't want to let her out of his sight.

So he lifted his coffee mug again, but instead of drinking from it, he only gazed down into its dark depths, as if he might find the answers to the mysteries of the universe lurking there. When he finally glanced up at Kirby again, he forced himself to return to his playful, flirtatious demeanor, even though playful and flirtatious were the last things he felt.

"So what you're telling me," he said softly, "is that if I was a local boy, you'd have no qualms about luring my interest. Is that it? Because if that's all it takes to get to know you intimately, then bring me a copy of the Yellow Pages quick. I can have a Realtor on the phone and become the boy next door—literally—in no time at all."

Kirby shook her head. "It's not that simple."

"Sounds simple enough to me."

"That's because you think money and notoriety can get you whatever you want."

His gaze was unwavering, his smile unfaltering as he assured her, "They can."

She shook her head dispiritedly. "Maybe in other parts of the world. But not here. Not in Endicott."

James felt less certain when he told her, "Yes, well, outside this little Brigadoon you call home, the world operates quite a bit differently."

"Which is exactly why I don't want to leave."

He smiled, but his heart wasn't in the gesture. "You never know, Kirby. You might like what you see out there."

She shook her head. "I like what I have here just fine, thanks."

Funny, but he was just beginning to realize that she dropped her gaze to the floor whenever she told a lie. "Now why do I have so much trouble believing that?" he wondered aloud.

She kept her eyes lowered as she told him, "Got me."

"Not yet, I don't. But I'm working on it."

"James..."

She sighed more than said his name, and he got the impression that it was because she just wasn't sure what she wanted to tell him. Finally, evidently, she decided that it might be best to just rewind and start the morning all over again. Because when at last she looked up and met his gaze, her eyes were distant, her posture indifferent, as if she were suffering from some kind of temporary amnesia.

What the hell, he thought. Might as well play along. They had weeks before they had to call the game on account of whether—whether or not she finally accepted that what had flared up between them was pretty much inescapable.

"So," she began with a halfhearted sigh, "you never said for sure. Are waffles okay for breakfast or not?"

James felt a buzz of warmth shudder through him at the mundane, thoroughly domestic, question. "Waffles sound great. What can I do to help?"

She seemed surprised by his offer, but she couldn't possibly be more surprised than he was to hear himself making it. Still, once uttered, he had no desire to take it back. Suddenly he wasn't at all averse to helping out in the kitchen, as long as he was assisting Chef Kirby. And as long as she didn't ask him to wear a frilly pink apron with cats on it.

Yet another first. His first time actually preparing breakfast. James had never made anything but reservations for a meal, and usually breakfast faded into lunch because he rarely rose from bed before noon. He didn't even bother to keep food in any of his homes, save the requisite industrial-size box of microwave popcorn and—it went without saying—a case of very good merlot.

He had expected his sojourn in bucolic Endicott, Indiana, to be filled with wonder and magic, but he'd thought Bob would be the one responsible for creating the spectacle. The comet had promised a once-in-a-decade-and-a-half experience, a feast for the eyes that would last a few weeks and provide a lifetime of awesome memories.

But instead of a comet, a slight blond woman who preferred baggy dresses and nude sunbathing was the one providing the wonder and magic. And so far, it was quite a show—one that surpassed the mere visual and tempted all the senses, one that could potentially last a lot longer than a few weeks.

Kirby had introduced him to a dozen new experiences already, and their relationship was only a few days old. How was he ever going to repay her, he wondered, for all of these first times he was coming to enjoy so much?

The moment the question unraveled in his brain, his libido— and other parts of his body that were best left undisturbed— jumped up with an answer. Maybe, just maybe, he thought, he could come up with a very good way to pay her back for all the first times to which she'd introduced him. Maybe, just maybe, there was a first time he could introduce her to, too.

And then, looking away to hide his smile from Kirby, he thought further that there was really no maybe about it.

"So, this is the grand marshal's float, huh?"

James settled a hand very gingerly on the papier-mâché monstrosity that was parked in a warehouse on the Endicott docks. Kirby had begun his official grand marshal's tour of the city by bringing him here, presumably to show off the, uh...the, um...the remarkable—yeah, it was certainly that—float that would be his throne for the three-hour duration of the Parallax Parade.

Outside the massive open door behind them, the muddy brown Ohio River flowed peacefully southwest, a direct contrast to the midmorning sky hanging bright blue above it. A warm breeze skittered into the warehouse and bounced around inside the cavernous tin room, nudging his unbound hair into his eyes. Automatically he tucked the unruly strands back behind his ears.

Four days had passed since he had agreed to become the centerpiece of the Welcome Back, Bob Comet Festival, and he was still trying to figure out just why he had agreed to do such a thing. Granted, his assigned baby-sitter had influenced his decision. But then, much to his irritation, Kirby had made it a point to keep a solid two car lengths between them whenever they found themselves together.

Which had turned out to be a lot less frequently than he had assumed it would be. Of course, had he been Rufus Laidlaw or Dierdre Mahoney, or some other homegrown phenomenon, Kirby probably would have been a much more constant companion. But *noooo.* Because he was James Nash, vagabond playboy, a man who struck terror in the hearts of virgins everywhere, she had somehow managed to renege on her festival committee obligations to keep the big-boy grand marshal entertained.

Until James had called her up and insisted she give him the respect due a grand marshal. He wanted a tour of the city, dammit. And he wanted it today.

Returning his attention to the float, he decided that, as thrones went, this one left a lot to be desired. Sitting on a tractor, its chicken-wire skeleton was only three-quarters covered with newspaper strips, watery glue and even more watery paint. Accessorized by the occasional tuft of toilet tissue or crepe paper steamer, it was obviously still a work in progress. The thing stood a good ten feet high, seemed in no way safe for habitation, and from what James could tell, it most closely resembled two huge red Las Vegas-style dice.

"Um, what exactly did you say the theme of the parade is?" he asked Kirby.

"'Life Is a Crap Shoot,'" she told him.

"Yes, well, I know that," he said, "but what's the theme of the parade?"

She narrowed her eyes at him some. "That *is* the theme. 'Life Is a Crap Shoot.' Mrs. Merwyn's fourth grade class won the Name-That-Parade-Theme contest. Their essay was by far the best."

James nodded and fought off the surreal feeling that threatened to wash over him every time he learned something new about Endicott, Indiana. "Fourth graders came up with that, did they?"

Kirby nodded.

"Gee, school sure has changed a lot since I was in fourth grade."

"Yeah, well, that's educational reform for you."

He was going to ask what "Life Is a Crap Shoot" had to do with returning comets, then decided he didn't want to know. Instead, he turned to Kirby and asked, "What big events do we have coming up for me to marshal grandly over?"

"Well, nothing until the parade Sunday," she told him.

He eyed the float again. "That's only two days away. Are you sure this thing will be finished by then?"

"I don't think they'll have a problem with it."

He turned his attention to Kirby then, and forced himself not to frown. Once again, she was dressed in something that looked to be an ill-fitting hand-me-down from her older sister, Laura Ashley Connaught. A big dress, with big sleeves, big pleats, big flowers, a big collar and a big bow. And little tiny flat shoes to go with.

Why did she insist on covering herself up with wallpaper, when he'd seen for himself what an incredible body she was hiding under that dress? It made no sense. Especially since she was clearly so intent on bagging herself a bachelor. If she thought her apparel was the kind of thing that turned a man on, then she was even more innocent than he'd thought.

"Well, since the parade is two days away," he began again, "it would appear that the two of us have a little time to call our own."

"Uh, did I mention I have a lunch date today?" she asked quickly. She glanced skittishly down at her watch and arched her brows in what was obviously faked surprise. "Gee, and in less than an hour, too. I totally forgot. I'm going to have to get going if I want to make it on time. We can do the city tour another day, 'kay?"

James was about to point out that it was just past 9:00 a.m., a tad early for lunch, even in the Central Time zone, but a loud *slam* halted the comment before he could utter it. As one, he and Kirby turned toward a door on the other side of the hangar, through which passed a tall, blond man wearing paint-spattered overalls and little else.

Uninterested in the newcomer, James turned his attention back to Kirby, only to find that she seemed to be anything *but* uninterested in the man's entrance. Instead, her cheeks had flushed that enchanting shade of pink that overcame them whenever she was embarrassed about something. Which, to James's way of thinking, seemed to be all the time.

"Hel-looo, Teddy," she sang out to the man, a shy smile playing about her lips.

James turned in time to see the newcomer spin around, the other man's expression indicating that he was obviously surprised to discover he wasn't alone. But when he saw Kirby standing there, he smiled back, the kind of smile that might overcome a proud father when he realizes his daughter has mastered perfectly the knee-in-the-groin maneuver he rehearsed with her prior to her first date.

"Hey, Kirby," the man identified as Teddy replied. He lifted his hand in greeting as he made his way across the room. "The float's coming along great, isn't it?"

Kirby nodded quickly, her gaze fixed on Teddy's face. Something in James's belly tightened fiercely when he saw her blush becomingly again. Okay, so the guy wasn't a bad-looking sort, he conceded. If you went for the blond, blue-eyed, Nordic god type who had great pecs and a golden tan. As far as James was concerned, though, that kind of perfection usually housed a truly boring personality. Of course, he thought further, that had never stopped him from being interested in such *women*, anyway, but still...

"I, ah..." Kirby began, stumbling over the simple sounds. She seemed to remember then that James was in the same area code, because she offered up a hasty introduction. "James, this is Teddy Gundersen. He's on the float committee. Teddy, this is James Nash."

"Mr. Gundersen," James greeted him formally.

"Oh, the grand marshal." Teddy nodded knowingly.

Yeah, and don't you forget it, pal, James thought, surprised by the uncharacteristic bout of attitude that suddenly overcame him.

"Nice to meet you," Teddy said pleasantly. Then he turned his attention back to Kirby. "So, what do you think of the float?"

Nervously she tucked a strand of that silky, near-white hair behind her ear, and James found himself wanting to reach out and put it back where it had been before, cascading carelessly over her shoulder. Instead, he clammed up tight and, like a young boy suffering his first crush, waited breathlessly to see what she would do next.

"You and the kids have done a terrific job," she told Teddy.

The other man turned to survey his handiwork and nodded. "Yeah, it's looking good. Should have it done by tomorrow with no problem."

Kirby nodded again, still obviously jittery as all get-out. "I'd really like to do something to show you my appreciation for all your hard work."

This time, Teddy shook his head. "It's not necessary. We've had fun with it. The kids have been great."

Kirby glanced up at him anxiously again. "No, I meant I'd like to do something to show *you* my appreciation," she said again, shifting the focus of her statement.

Teddy shrugged. "That's okay, Kirb. Like I said, we've all had—"

"No," Kirby interrupted emphatically, "I want to show *you* my appreciation. Not the kids. You."

"But the kids—"

"How about I fix you dinner at my place? Next week?" she asked eagerly.

James found himself wanting to applaud with vigor when the other man finally seemed to understand what Kirby was trying to get at. Unfortunately, the haunted, hunted look that overcame Teddy was reward enough for James.

"Oh. I see. Uh...thanks, Kirb, but I, uh...I don't think it's necessary."

"But I'd like to do *some*thing to show you my gratitude. I could cook dinner for you, and then we could—"

"No! Not dinner!" Teddy insisted as he began to back up, wariness overcoming him with each step he took.

"But I want to—"

"No!" he shouted more adamantly, throwing his hands up, palms out before him, as if he were trying to ward off a blow to his manhood. "Really, you don't have to."

"But, Teddy—"

"I, uh, I have to go."

GET A FREE TEDDY BEAR...

You'll love this plush, cuddly Teddy Bear, an adorable accessory for your dressing table, bookcase or desk. Measuring 5 ½" tall, he's soft and brown and has a bright red ribbon around his neck – he's completely captivating! And he's yours *absolutely free*, when you accept this no-risk offer!

► CLAIM YOUR FREE BOOKS AND FREE GIFT! RETURN THIS CARD TODAY! ►

NO OBLIGATION TO BUY!

And without another word, the Thor-like Mr. Gundersen was off, fleeing back through the door through which he'd entered, the click of what could only be a deadbolt being thrust into place a solid exclamation point that punctuated his escape. And then Kirby and James were alone in the big hangar once again. For a moment, neither of them spoke of what had just transpired. Unfortunately, seeing as how he had never been one for discretion, James found that he simply could not let the episode pass without comment.

"You know," he began, his voice low and speculative, "your MO could stand a lot of improvement."

"My MO?" Kirby echoed absently, her gaze still trained on the door through which her quarry had escaped.

"Your Method of Operation," James elaborated. "It is, in a word, *lousy.*"

At that, she returned her attention to him fully. "I don't know what you're talking about," she said coolly.

"You'll never land yourself a man the way you're going about it," he told her. "It's all wrong."

She spun around to face him, settled her hands on her hips in challenge and glared at him. "I wasn't trying to 'operate,' as you put it, anything with Teddy. Or any other man in town, for that matter."

James threw his arms wide. "Come on, Kirby," he cajoled. "I've seen you operate. I've seen the casualties you've left behind. I've heard the gossip, and you yourself have confessed to a variety of sordid acts of procurement."

She gasped, her indignation an almost palpable thing. "Procurement? How dare you suggest such a thing!"

"Oh, do pardon me," he said without an ounce of apology in his voice. "I didn't mean to *suggest* anything. I thought I was being pretty forthright."

Her response to that was to throw him a look that was positively simmering.

James wasn't sure what had come over him to make him speak so meanly to Kirby. He only knew that having watched her turn on the charm for some undeserving jerk like Teddy—who didn't even realize what a veritable feast of erotica he had just turned down—when she continued to keep James at arm's length, made him feel just a tiny bit perturbed.

"Oh, and I suppose *you're* such an expert on the subject of landing men?" she demanded.

He hoped he didn't look too smug as he replied, "Well, yes, as a matter of fact, I am."

"You've landed a lot of men in your day, have you?"

"No. But I've been landed myself on a number of occasions. And I guarantee you, the women who reeled me in could have run rings around you as hunter-gatherers."

Great. This was just what she needed, Kirby thought. James Nash, a man whose prerequisites for finding a woman attractive could fill a peanut shell, was now telling her she didn't stand a chance of ever charming a man into her...um, house. First Teddy running in terror from her dinner invitation, now this. And it wasn't even midmorning yet. Could this day possibly get any worse?

"I could offer you a few tips, you know," James told her, interrupting what had promised to be a really nice bout of self-pity.

Oh, yes, she thought further when she heard his offer. This day could definitely get worse. "Who says I need any tips?" she asked petulantly.

He grinned playfully. "Well, there are probably plenty of part-time people at the Peter Piper Pickle Plant we could probe for preliminary preponderance."

She frowned at him. "Meaning?"

"Meaning all those poor saps you've tried to lure—"

"I told you," she interrupted, "that I have *not* tried to *lure* any—"

"I'm sure they could all shed some light on your technique," James finished easily. "However, since all of them appear to quake in fear at the very idea of being left alone in the same room with you, you're going to have to rely on me instead."

She felt her outrage slipping some at the smile that softened his words. Darn him. For a promiscuous playboy Peeping Tom, he really did have a way with delivery. "You think you can help me with my technique," she repeated, assuring herself she was *not* really interested in what he had to say.

"I know I can."

Wondering why she bothered to even continue the conversation, Kirby nonetheless found herself adding, "I wasn't aware that I even had a 'technique.'"

James made a face at her. "Believe me. After witnessing that little display with Mr. Gundersen, I guarantee, you have a technique." He paused a telling moment before adding, "It's just not a very good one."

Kirby lifted her chin an indignant fraction of an inch. "I beg your pardon, but I don't think—"

"Luckily for you, however," he interrupted her easily, "you have at your disposal someone who's very good at perfecting techniques."

"Yes, well, as I tried to tell you I don't—"

"But before we do anything else, that dress has got to go."

Six

Well, that certainly cut off any argument Kirby might have been ready to utter. *"What?"*

Unfortunately, James was ignoring her objections completely, too caught up had he obviously become in considering her from head to toe. "Yeah," he finally decided with a confident nod, "that dress is just going to have to come off. And as my father used to always tell me, there's no time like the present."

Kirby could only stare at him dumbfounded. He wanted her to take off her dress? Why? Well, of course she already knew *why.* He'd made that clear enough over the past few days. But here? Now?

"Not here. Not now," he said with a chuckle, as if he'd read her thoughts and found them laughable. When she continued to only gaze at him in completely befuddled silence, he smiled and added, "Come on. I'll show you."

The next thing she knew, Kirby was sitting in the back of James's Rolls-Royce, a roomy compartment redolent of leather interior. With a flick of a switch, one of the Brandenburg Concertos erupted from the speakers behind and beside her, and a smoked glass screen rose between the two of them and their driver.

James sat on the expansive cream-colored leather seat beside her with more confidence than anyone had a right to claim. Dressed in sapphire blue trousers and a white linen, collarless shirt, his black hair skimming his shoulders like silk, he was more handsome than she'd ever seen him looking.

Worse than that, however, he was studying her with more interest than she was comfortable acknowledging. She suddenly felt as if he were a womanizing Hollywood producer who had plans, big plans, to make her a star, a big star. But first, a little side trip to the casting couch.

"Yeah, that dress has got to go," he reiterated, scanning her body from the tips of her pale blue flats to the beribboned lace of her big, white collar.

In an instinctive act of self-preservation, Kirby lifted her hand to the blue satin bow that topped a good three dozen pearl buttons. "I don't think so," she told him. "This is one of my favorite dresses."

"I can't begin to imagine why."

His offhand comment stung her fiercely, even though she told herself it didn't matter. What did she care if he liked her dress or not? Anyone who would furnish his home with animal-skin prints had about as much fashion sense as Tarzan anyway.

In spite of that, she found herself asking, "What's wrong with this dress?"

"Not a thing," he told her. "If you happen to be six years old and on your way to church for Easter services. But you're a grown woman, Kirby, trying to attract a grown man. And you're going about it all wrong."

She supposed it would be pointless to deny yet again that she was trying to lure a man, especially after James had just witnessed her attempted, um...oh, what the heck—she might as well admit it—her attempted *luring* of Teddy Gundersen.

Still, he didn't have to make it sound so tawdry. The way he spoke of her behavior made her feel like her only goal in life was to get a man into her bedroom. In fact, she wanted one in her bedroom, her kitchen, her bathroom, her living room, her backyard, her storage shed and her garage. Not a man for each room, of course, but one man to occupy them all, depending on where he was most needed.

"Okay, look." She relented some. "I suppose there's no sense in trying to convince you otherwise, especially when I told you that my one wish for Bob was to bring me a man who would love me forever. I do want a man. But not the way you keep insisting I want one. There's a lot more to a relationship than sex."

"Maybe. Maybe not." James's expression was inscrutable as he uttered the comment. "But the fact remains that for the kind of relationship you want—namely marital—there's a very good chance that there's going to be *some* sex involved. I don't know how much your mother told you about the facts of life, but if you want those kids..."

She frowned. "Well, I do know where babies come from."

He had the nerve to actually look surprised. "Do you? Wonderful. That will make this thing so much easier."

"What thing?"

The moment she asked the question, Kirby wished she hadn't. Something in his eyes was just too...calculating for her comfort.

James leaned forward, propped his elbows on his knees and steepled his fingers thoughtfully together. "Kirby, my dear," he said intently, as he turned his head to look at her, "we're going to catch you a man. One who will at least make a show of loving you forever, if that's what you really want. One who will play stud to that passel of rugrats you seem to desire so badly. One who will sit on that porch swing of yours with you well into your golden years."

He frowned as if he'd just swallowed something that tasted really awful. "Though why you'd want such a thing is beyond me."

She ignored the last part of his statement, stored the first part for future commentary and focused on the middle part for now. "What do you mean he'll 'at least make a show of loving me forever'?"

He emitted a half chuckle, as if she were joking. "Surely you weren't serious about that love forever-after stuff, were you?"

"Of course I was serious. Why wouldn't I be serious about something so serious?"

His response was another of those annoying little half-humorous sounds, followed by, "Because there's no such thing, that's why."

"Of course there's such a thing," she insisted.

"I've never seen it."

"That's hardly surprising, considering the kind of social circle you surround yourself with. But I assure you, Mr. Nash, that such an emotion definitely exists, and that most normal people have experienced it at least once."

He smiled indulgently. "Listen to yourself. Most people have experienced a forever-after kind of love *at least once?* That makes no sense. If it lasted forever, they'd *never* experience it more than once, would they?"

"That's not what I meant."

"Then, please, by all means, clarify yourself."

Kirby dipped her head and found her gaze settling on the two hands she had entwined nervously in her lap. On the fourth finger of her right hand, she wore an engagement ring, the one her father had given to her mother thirty-five years ago. She was confident that had they lived, her parents would have remained devotedly in love well into their golden years and beyond. Like Angie's parents would. Like Rosemary's would have if her father had lived. Like all her friends' parents in Endicott.

She couldn't remember having a single childhood buddy who had come from a broken home. A lot of that, no doubt, was because Endicott was a small, conservative, midwestern town where things like divorce just weren't the norm. But a lot of it was because, at least in Endicott, people fell in love forever. It was a serious thing, love, not to be taken lightly. But to people like James, she supposed that falling in and out of love was just another way to pass the time while you waited for happy hour to begin again.

"I just meant," she said, "that no matter who we wind up spending the rest of our lives with, nearly everyone has one grand passion in their lifetime. Someone they know they'll never forget, someone whose face rises up out of nowhere to haunt them when they least expect it, someone whose voice, whose scent, whose...whose *feel* jars them out of a deep sleep for scores of nights to come, and keeps them wakeful and wanting until dawn.''

She looked over to meet James's gaze, but found that neither his eyes, nor his expression, revealed a clue as to what he might be thinking. So she went on. "Maybe it's not the person they marry, or even the person they grow old with. But it's there. A forever-after kind of love. Someone you can never forget. It hits everybody at some point in their life, and they never quite recover.''

"It's never hit me," he replied quickly, certainly.

Kirby couldn't help the sad smile that curled her lips. "Not yet," she said.

He shook his head resolutely. "And it never will."

"How can you be so sure?"

"Because that kind of thing just doesn't exist."

"How do you know?"

"I just do."

"Yeah, but how?"

The good-humored, indulgent smile that had played about his mouth suddenly turned sour. "I just do," he repeated emphatically. Then, swiftly and easily he turned the tables. "But we were discussing you."

"Actually, *you* were discussing me," she corrected him. "I really have no idea what you've been going on about."

"I told you. We're going to catch you a man. If Bob won't bring you one, we'll just have to take matters into our own hands."

"We?" she repeated, an uneasy suspicion unwinding in her belly. "Why we?"

"Because, Kirby, you can't do this without me. I'm going to provide the one essential ingredient that will ensure the success of this endeavor."

She hated to think what that essential ingredient might be. Which was why she didn't ask him to elaborate. "I'm not sure this is such a good idea," she allowed instead.

"Of course it's a good idea. Trust me. Now," he continued

quickly when she opened her mouth to object again, "where do you do your clothes shopping?"

She eyed him warily for a moment before answering, "A little boutique in downtown Endicott called Rose's Romantic Reminiscences."

"Fine." He punched his thumb against a button on the wall to the left of his head. "Omar?"

There was a brief click, then the driver's voice acknowledging, "Yes, Mr. Nash?"

James sighed heavily, as if in put-upon patience. "How many times do I have to ask? Will you please call me 'James'?" he told the other man.

"Whatever you say, Mr. Nash."

James rolled his eyes heavenward, then said, "Omar, if you see a shop in town called Rose's Romantic Reminiscences, floor the accelerator and speed past it as quickly as you possibly can, okay?"

Somehow Kirby managed to refrain from comment.

"Yes, Mr. Nash," the driver replied.

"James," he said adamantly into the speaker. "It's *James*."

"Yes, Mr. Nash."

He grumbled, but released the button on the intercom without further comment. "Now, then," he continued as he dropped his hand back to the seat, "where do all the college girls do their clothes shopping?"

She was tempted to tell him that she had absolutely no idea, having never been a college girl herself, but unfortunately, Kirby knew full well where all the young, hip women in town shopped. She knew because it was right across the street from her own office in town, and since she never seemed to have any work to do, she spent many a day gazing out the window marveling at some of the things women would put on their bodies these days.

"At a place called Wild Life," she told James reluctantly. "It's at the corner of Third and Main."

He pushed the button again and directed his driver to hie them to the location, buzzing off with an emphatic, "And step on it."

"Yes, Mr. Nash."

"James," he corrected his driver. "*James.*"

"Yes, sir."

James opened his mouth and was about to push the button again, then seemed to think better of arguing. Instead, he met Kirby's gaze levelly again and told her, "Forget about the city tour. Today we're going shopping. We need a little bait for that man trap we're going to set."

"James, I really don't think this is such a good idea."

James absorbed the sight of the new and improved Kirby "Man-Killer" Connaught, who stood front and center in her living room, and he decided immediately that her comment was right on target.

However, she undoubtedly thought this was a bad idea for entirely different reasons than he did. She probably wasn't comfortable in the snug red miniskirt hugging her hips and the snugger, redder cropped tank top embracing her torso. And the red high-heeled sandals and big red hoop earrings would also doubtless take some getting used to.

Likewise, he wasn't exactly comfortable with Kirby's ensemble, either. As he'd absorbed the sight of her in her new duds, parts of his body that he hadn't realized could tighten and heat had tightened and heated up. And it had come as a major shock to discover that a woman could actually be even sexier *with* clothes on than she was without. Because the sight of Kirby naked as a jaybird paled when juxtaposed to the sight of her all gussied up like a howling red siren.

"Oh, I don't know," he said evasively, cupping his hand to his forehead as if testing for a fever. "It's not *that* bad an idea."

She crossed her arms over her breasts in a clear effort to conceal herself, an effort that was totally, thankfully, ineffective. "But I *never* wear stuff like this," she objected. "My *underwear* is more substantial than this stuff." She blushed, "That is, my old underwear was. The underwear you made me buy today, well..."

James swallowed hard, forced himself to glance away from the soft swell of her breasts that had peeked out of her top and tried not think about Kirby's new underwear. "That, uh..." He cleared his throat indelicately and tried again. "That's the point, Kirby. That's also the reason you've never snagged a husband."

"Oh, come on. You can't tell me that my inability to interest a man is based solely on my wardrobe. No man is that superficial. Not even you," she added pointedly.

"Hey, I can be plenty superficial," he assured her dryly. "But you're right. There's more to attracting a man than a short skirt and a tight shirt, although those definitely head the list of any healthy, red-blooded American man's requirements in a mate."

She shook her head in obvious disappointment. "You are *so* out of touch with reality."

"*I'm* out of touch with reality?" he sputtered. "Excuse me? *I'm* not the one who grew up in a Thornton Wilder play starring Debbie Reynolds. Talk about unreality."

"No, you no doubt grew up as Pauly Shore starring in some low-budget, drive-in flick called *Sorority Babes in Kneesocks*," she shot back. Then, before he had a chance to retort, she changed the subject with a swift glance down at her apparel. "I still can't believe I let you talk me into this."

Frankly, James couldn't believe it, either. But there had been times that afternoon when Kirby had almost seemed like she was having fun with the transformation. The salesgirl at Wild Life— he hesitated to call her a woman, because she couldn't have been more than sixteen—had been enormously helpful, though extremely surprised, when they had walked through the door. And not because he was James Nash, Cultural American Icon, either. It was because the girl was a student in the Sunday school class Kirby taught, and she hadn't realized her teacher of Psalms and Proverbs harbored such a wild streak.

Then again, some of those Psalms and Proverbs got kinda racy sometimes, James recalled with a fond smile.

Of course, Kirby *didn't* house a wild streak at all, he reminded himself quickly, corralling his thoughts before they could bolt from the gate. Even so, although James had been the one to select her new wardrobe, that hadn't prevented her from becoming utterly renewed by the simple transition from Laura *Ash*ley to Gypsy *Rose* Lee.

"You let me talk you into this," he told her, "because you

know your own efforts to find a husband have failed miserably. Comet Bob or no Comet Bob, I'm the closest thing you've got to wish fulfillment right now. So with that in mind, what should we do tonight?''

Her eyebrows shot up in surprise, presumably at the speedy change in subject matter. ''Speaking for myself,'' she said, jabbing a thumb over her shoulder, ''I'm going to go back into my bedroom and take off this ridiculous outfit.''

James reached for the top button of his shirt and quickly unfastened it. ''Sounds like a great plan to me,'' he told her, moving down to the next button with equal zeal. ''I was going to save that particular lesson until later, but hey, if you're so anxious to jump ahead in your studies, well, far be it from me to—''

''No!'' she cried when she saw what he was doing. ''I didn't mean you were going to take off your clothes, too! Just me!''

He expelled a quiet sound of disappointment, feigning surprise. ''Well, where's the fun in that?''

''James, I mean it, if you don't button yourself back up right now—''

''At least you're back to using my first name again.'' He interrupted her pique before it had a chance to cut loose. Still, he didn't follow her instructions to refasten his buttons. It had, after all, suddenly become rather warm in the room. ''Maybe there's hope for you yet.''

Instead of answering, she sulkily crossed her arms over her midsection again, and again, his gaze was drawn to the top of her shirt, where the creamy curves of her breasts were just begging to be cupped by a lover's hands. At least she didn't leave the room as she'd threatened. He didn't know if that was because she was really interested in carrying out their plan, or because she was afraid he'd follow her. Either way, it worked to keep her close.

''Now, then,'' he began again, running a tongue over his suddenly dry lips, ''where's the best place to go in town to meet single men?''

She thought for a moment, then answered, ''The library?''

James closed his eyes and shook his head.

''Church?'' she asked further.

He squeezed his eyes shut tighter. "Uh, no. Guess again."

"The grocery store?"

"No-o..."

When she said nothing more, he opened his eyes to find her nibbling her lip with much thought, her eyes narrowed in concentration. "Oh, I know," she finally piped up, snapping her fingers. "Peterson Booksellers holds these singles' nights the second Wednesday of every month."

James sighed wearily. "No. Try again."

She nodded knowingly. "I guess you're right. This isn't the second Wednesday of the month." She returned to her earlier posture of impending brain strain, obviously clueless about where to go to meet men.

Finally taking pity on her, James said, "Bars, Kirby. Bars are the best place to meet men."

"Oh, no," she assured him. "That can't be right. Why would I go to a bar to meet a man? I'm not a recreational drinker."

He recalled that pilfered bottle of Perrier-Jouët that must be chilling somewhere in her refrigerator—at least, he hoped it was chilling in her refrigerator, because it really messed up wine to be chilled then warmed then chilled once again—but he remained stoically silent on the subject.

"No, really, Kirby," he said instead, "bars are a good place to meet people. Honest."

She still didn't look convinced. "Really?"

"Really."

"Gee, how about that? I never knew."

As had become habitual when dealing with Kirby, James wondered if he was dreaming. She had claimed to have girlfriends. This Angie person who wrote about crime waves where there were none, and this Rosemary person who had some unfathomable history with someone Kirby had deemed a "pizza-faced little twerp." What kind of friends were they to have allowed her to grow up with such mind-numbing misconceptions about life? Then again, if they were friends of Kirby's—and if they'd grown up in Endicott—who was to say they weren't similarly victims of extended adolescence?

"So can you recommend a bar that might attract a crowd of single men?" he asked, wondering why he bothered.

"Well, let's see now.... Bars...bars...bars..." She thought for a moment, pressing her index finger to her lips, smudging the scarlet lipstick that was another trophy of their earlier hunt for red enticement.

"Kirby," James groaned when he realized what she had done. "You've smeared your lipstick."

Immediately she jerked her hand away from her mouth, frowning at the stain of red on her finger. "Oh, no. I'm sorry. I'm just not used to wearing it." She reached up again, striving to repair the damage, but her efforts only made it worse.

James reached into his pocket for a handkerchief and crossed the room to where she stood. "Here, let me," he offered quietly.

Deciding that it would probably be best for her to just go back and reapply the color, he swiped gently at her mouth until the lipstick was completely gone. And when it was, when he saw her slightly parted and very naked lips right there close at hand, something came over him unlike anything he'd ever experienced before.

Uncontrollable desire. *Uncontrollable* desire. He'd never lost control in his entire life. Never. Until now. Until he saw Kirby standing there, ripe for the picking, her eyes full of trusting and wanting and needing...and something else he was afraid to identify. And before he even realized what he was doing, he bent his head and grazed his mouth lightly over hers.

Just one little kiss, he promised himself. That's all he would take, all he would need to satisfy his curiosity about the taste of her, the feel of her. And true to his word, James only skimmed his slightly parted lips over hers softly, swiftly, sweetly. She was like spun sugar, he thought vaguely as he started to pull back, and he could easily grow addicted to such a treat. He halted before moving completely away, drawn by the way her warm breath mingled with his, and the way her respiration seemed to have suddenly quickened in time with his own.

Okay, two little kisses, he amended suddenly. One more couldn't possibly hurt.

This time he took a step closer, curled a finger under her chin and gently tipped her head backward. Her gaze met his, her eyes blue and beckoning and bottomless, and suddenly he felt as if the control he'd lost would never return. Neither of them spoke as he bent his head toward her again. But this time when he did, James took possession. He spread his free hand open over her back, leaned in over her, pressed her backward and covered her mouth with his.

Magical. That was what it seemed to be when he kissed Kirby the second time. Some warm, fizzy, incoherent sensation swept over him, like a cloud filled with buzzing energy. And once he started kissing her, he found that he just couldn't stop. So he cupped her jaw, knifed his fingers through her hair and tilted her head back to deepen the kiss.

Vaguely he noted that she didn't do anything to stop him. Vaguely he realized that she seemed to be joining in quite nicely, thanks. Vaguely he felt himself slipping away, into some kind of hazy erogenous zone he'd never visited before. Her mouth under his was warm, willing, wonderful. So what could he do but kiss her again? And again. And again. And again...

And as he kissed her, James took another step closer, bringing her body flush against his. The hand he had woven in her hair slipped down to her nape, cupping the slender column lovingly. She tasted...so sweet. And she felt...so soft. And she smelled...so sexy. And all he could do was fall deeper and deeper into the darkness of his senses, to find himself wandering blindly in a part of himself he'd never visited before.

Incandescent. That was how it felt to finally, finally, have Kirby in his arms. Their bodies seemed to melt together, to fuse into one, to unite as a single entity. Beneath his fingers, her bare shoulder was hot to the touch, and he found himself wondering if she was that feverish all over. So he skimmed his other hand lower, down along the soft fabric of her shirt, until he located her bare back beneath.

Oh, yes. She was hot there, too. He spread his fingers wide over her soft flesh, dipping his thumb under the hem of her shirt and his little finger into the waistband of her skirt. Then he urged her closer still, opening his legs to press her firmly against him.

One of them groaned at the intimate contact, though James

never was sure who, but neither of them made any effort to stop the chemical reaction that threatened to burn them both down to their cores. He felt Kirby's fingers in his hair, skimming tentatively at first, then gradually burrowing more insistently, more possessively. He moved his hand from her shoulder to her throat, to the gentle hollow at its base. Then he sent his lips following the path of his fingers, and he tasted the slender column and soft cleft before skimming his open mouth over her shoulders.

"Oh, James," Kirby whispered, dropping her head back.

He took advantage of her, offering to taste her neck again, moving his hands to her hips, pulling her forward for a more thorough exploration. When still she made no effort to protest, he grew bolder, skimming his hands over the elegant swell of her derriere, cupping her gently in his palms, urging her as insistently against himself as he dared.

"Oh, *James...*" she echoed more breathlessly.

He ripened to attention against her belly, a development she had to recognize, regardless of her innocence. He waited for her to faint dead away at the evidence of his arousal—surely her virginal sensibilities were by now far too overwrought to continue with what they were doing—but she only moved a little to her left, then a little to her right, as if trying to accommodate him better.

The subtle friction was nearly his undoing.

Back off, James, he commanded himself. He knew he should go slow with Kirby, but every base, primitive instinct inside him was clamoring for him to end the erotic onslaught *now* and take what she was offering. Then he remembered that she couldn't possibly even understand what she was offering, having never offered it before. So he scaled back his attack some, buried his face in the soft skin of her neck and forced himself to slow down.

The scent of her nearly overwhelmed him, though, that hint of sweet lavender that only a woman like her could pull off. He filled his lungs with her fragrance, holding his breath in an effort to preserve her memory forever. Then, growing dizzy with the inhalation, he reluctantly released it, confident that he would store reminders of her elsewhere instead.

And then that thought, too, was gone, because Kirby circled

one hand behind his neck and dropped her other to his chest, splaying her fingers gently over the heart that was raging behind his ribs. Her touch was so innocent, so artless, so incredibly tentative that he groaned aloud at the simple caress. He couldn't ever recall feeling quite the way Kirby made him feel. And he was both astounded and terrified at the realization.

"Kirby," he whispered softly, afraid somehow, that by saying her name too loudly, the spell would be broken, and she might dissolve in his arms.

"Hmm?" she murmured, the sound a mixture of needing and wanting.

"I, uh..."

He drew in a deep breath and released it slowly before venturing further. Then he straightened some, to touch his forehead to hers. For a long moment, all he could do was stand there holding her, skimming his hands languidly over her taut fanny, reveling in her nearness, in her desire and need. Then he closed his eyes, curled his fingers more insistently into her soft skin, and pulled her closer still.

"Oh..." she murmured again, this time so quietly, he barely heard the sound. And as she had before, she responded instinctively, with a subtle move of her body that hinted at a much more intimate joining.

"Like I said—" he tried again as a spiral of heat wound through him "—I had kind of planned on saving this lesson for later, but if it means that much to you to jump right in this way..."

His softly uttered words were like ice water on a candle. Immediately Kirby's dreamy-eyed desire flickered out completely. Her eyes snapped open, a swirl of anger and betrayal clouding their normally clear blue depths. The fingers she had opened so eagerly upon him suddenly curled shut tight, and she rested her fists on his chest for only a moment before pushing hard to propel him away. But James didn't want to go away, so he stood firm, gripping her at the waist, holding her close.

"James, let me go," she hissed, the quiet words hitting him with the force of a Mack truck.

For one wild, delirious moment, he honestly thought about ignoring her request and feeding his own hunger instead. That's how greedy he'd become where Kirby was concerned. Then, calling himself a fool, he released her, pushing her gently away.

"Sorry," he bit off curtly, feeling in no way apologetic. "I should have realized that lesson was far too advanced for you right now."

When he let her go, she covered her mouth with loosely curled fingers, as if she were trying to protect a tender wound. "I think I just need a...a different teacher," she muttered from behind her hand. "The lesson itself was...was..."

He held his breath as he asked softly, "Was what?"

But she just shook her head and said nothing more.

He tried to smile, but felt too raw and brittle inside to accomplish it. Kirby learning that particular lesson from another instructor was something James didn't want to think about right now. So he did his best to pretend it didn't matter, and went back to playing his part.

"Well, we'll just put that lesson off for another day, then," he said. "For now, there are still a few things we haven't covered with your new makeover."

She shook her head slowly, her eyes still dark with confusion. "Like I told you. I don't think this is such a good idea. I think I've changed my mind about letting you help me out."

He swallowed the panic that rose in his throat at hearing himself dismissed so easily. "You need me, Kirby. You need my help. You know you do."

"Your 'help,' as you call it, is the *last* thing I need. I was doing just fine until you came along."

"Were you?"

Again she didn't answer, just continued to meet his gaze silently.

He drew in another deep breath, waited until he felt his heartbeat slow down, then expelled it slowly. "What if I promise you that nothing like what just happened will ever happen again?"

She eyed him warily. "What if I don't trust you on that particular promise?"

"Or maybe it's that you don't trust yourself?" he asked further, unable to help himself.

She only glared at him in response.

He relented some at that. "Look, I may be a lot of things, Kirby, but I'm not one to go back on my word. And I'm certainly not one to try and make a woman do something she doesn't want to do. I can promise you that nothing like what just happened will happen again." He hesitated deliberately before adding, "Not until you want it to."

"Oh, I think it's pretty safe to say I'm not going to want it to."

"Fine. If that winds up being your decision, then that's the way it will be. In the meantime, we still have a few things to address if we want to lure some unsuspecting sap into your web."

For a moment, he thought she was going to maintain her position on the matter and tell him to take a hike. She remained stony and silent, as if she were trying to predict in advance each and every step their project would take, so that she could plan her counterattack in advance.

Good luck, James thought. Because although he'd been the one to choose the path, even *he* couldn't say where the road they were about to travel would ultimately lead them.

Finally, when he thought she would say nothing more, she asked cautiously, "What kind of things?"

Grateful for the reprieve, and wanting to seize it before she changed her mind, James mentally scanned his Kirby to-do list. Gee, where to begin... Finally he surrendered and decided that with her wardrobe situation rectified at last, they might as well just move along to the next major obstacle they had facing them.

"Your reputation, for one," he said plainly.

Confusion colored her expression. "My reputation?"

He nodded. "Yes. Unfortunately, your reputation in this town is spotless."

She smiled uncertainly. "I know. I've worked hard to keep it that way. So?"

"So we're just going to have to do something about that, aren't we?"

She chewed her lip thoughtfully for a moment. "Um, like what?"

"Kirby," James said, rocking back on his heels with all the

confidence of Professor Henry Higgins, "I'm afraid it's going to be necessary to ruin your good reputation in Endicott."

She dropped her hand from her mouth to gape at him, but she said nothing more.

So he leaned forward, as if his body were somehow instinctively drawn toward hers. "The reason none of the available men in town are interested in getting romantically involved with you isn't because you're unattractive."

She seemed to brighten some at that. "I'm not?"

Oh, boy, was she clueless, James thought. "No. Trust me. You are definitely *not* an unattractive woman. It's your lily-white reputation, your unsullied status that's keeping the men in this town at bay. No man wants to be responsible for deflowering such a delicate blossom as you."

Well, most men wouldn't, he amended. James himself discovered much to his surprise that he found the whole idea to be rather...startlingly...explosively... He sighed raggedly. Arousing as hell.

"So what are we going to do?" she asked, her quiet voice dragging him back from the illicit ideas parading across the forefront of his brain.

"Hmm?" he asked with much distraction.

"My reputation," she reminded him. "You said it's too good."

"That's right." He remembered now. He began again. "As I said, somebody is going to have to do something to ruin your reputation in Endicott." Then, indulging in his biggest, broadest bad boy smile, he added, "And I'm just the guy to do it."

Seven

Kirby didn't much care for the way James was suddenly looking at her—as if he were the biggest, baddest, meanest alley cat on the block, and she were Fifi, the world champion Angora, who had been inadvertently left out in the rain.

"Uh…" she began eloquently. "Ruin my reputation?" She felt her face flame, but was helpless to add, "Isn't that what you just tried to do a few minutes ago?"

His eyes lit up at the reminder, with a glittering fire the source of which she didn't even want to consider. "Yes, well," he said as he took a few casual steps forward, "that was with rather inconclusive results, wasn't it? Besides," he added hastily, "it wasn't available for public consumption. And public displays are going to be imperative from here on out."

She wasn't sure she understood him exactly. "What do you mean?"

"I mean if we're going to ruin your reputation—and believe me, Kirby, I intend to leave it in tatters—then we're going to have to make sure that every available man in Endicott knows without a doubt that the delicate little flower known as Kirby Connaught has been finally—and thoroughly—plucked.''

This time, instead of flaring with the heat of embarrassment, she felt her face go pale from the loss of blood. "You're going to...pluck me?"

He smiled that roguish smile again. "Not unless you want me to. And not unless you ask me nicely. Mainly, what we want to do is make sure the men in this town *think* that I've plucked you. As many times as possible, too. Once they know someone else has done the hard part—if you'll pardon the incredibly tacky pun—then they'll line up for a piece of the action."

"They will?"

He nodded carelessly. "It's a guy thing."

She frowned. "But that makes men sound so...so cheap. So...tawdry. So easy."

He shrugged. "Hey, if the shoe fits..."

Kirby was liking less and less the turn this conversation had taken. "I don't know..." she began, her voice trailing off as uncertainly as her convictions were. Suddenly, the idea of trying to attract the men in her hometown wasn't nearly as appealing as it had been before.

Before James had entered the picture.

She told herself that was only because James had offered her insight into the male animal that she'd never had before, and now the male animal seemed to be just that—an animal. Did she honestly want to get any closer to such a creature than she absolutely had to? And on purpose, at that? What had once been her most fervent dream—to have a local boy fall in love with her forever—suddenly didn't seem nearly as...well, dreamy, as it had once been.

"You really think it's necessary to ruin my reputation?"

He nodded fiercely. "It's absolutely essential."

"Gee, I don't know..."

Despite the fact that he was basically only seconding what Angie and Rosemary had already told her, Kirby thought long and hard before responding further.

Just what on earth had happened between the two of them earlier, she wondered? One minute, James had been wiping the smudged lipstick off her mouth, and the next minute, she'd been cashing in a one-way ticket to the magic land of Erotica. She'd never known how it could be with a man. She'd never realized how much heat, how much power, how much desire the human body and brain could generate with just a few simple touches.

She'd heard the term "sparks fly" often enough in her life. But when she and James had rubbed against each other, they'd created a friction that bypassed sparks completely and went straight to atomic meltdown. And if the hot, shuddering sensations she'd just experienced had come from only a couple of kisses and a few well-placed touches, then what would happen to her if the two of them got around to actually...actually...um...

Strangely, she found herself wanting desperately to find out.

"Your choice, Kirby," she heard James say.

She returned her gaze to his face, taking in the gray eyes that had looked upon her in both humor and need, at the mouth that had smiled at her, frowned at her and wreaked havoc on her senses. James had been fairly easy to read from the start, never bothering to hide his thoughts or opinions from her, letting her know in no uncertain terms *exactly* how he felt. Right now, however, his expression was completely impassive, and his face revealed nothing of what he might be thinking.

Had Angie and Rosemary been right when they'd echoed exactly what James was telling her now? Could it be true that her problem in attracting a man was simply that she was too sweet and innocent for any of them to want to sully her?

In spite of what everyone in Endicott seemed to believe, Kirby was experienced enough to know that there was no longer a premium on goodness and innocence that there had been once upon a time. But she hadn't thought that those two qualities might have been cast so far by the wayside that they were now considered drawbacks in a person's character. Certainly she didn't expect to be *prized* for her personal choices in this day and age, but she hadn't expected to be ostracized for them, either.

Yet she'd seen for herself how reluctant the men of Endicott were to get to know her better. Angie and Rosemary and James must know what they were talking about, if all of them had arrived at their conclusions independently. Their reasoning was as good as any, Kirby supposed, because she couldn't come up with any explanation at all for her romantic solitude.

"What's it going to be, Kirby?"

James's question jarred her out of her musings, but she still had no idea how to answer him. So she only gazed at him in silence, feeling more and more confused and dispirited with every passing moment.

"If you want to remain Endicott's vestal virgin for the rest of your life," he began again, apparently heartened by her lack of response, "then you can throw me out of your house right now. You can take your credit card back to Rose's Romantic Reminiscences and buy all the buttons and bows you want. You can hide out in the library and pretend you couldn't care less about the world around you. And you can watch the fleeing backs of men for the rest of your life.

"However," he added, taking a few steps toward her to eliminate the distance she had created between them. This time she didn't move away. "If you want to take a little walk on the wild side..." He came to a stop immediately in front of her. "If you want to know how good it feels to be bad... If you have a single hope in hell of ever experiencing that singular ecstasy that explodes between a man and a woman..."

She lifted her gaze to his, only barely catching herself before she fell right into the dangerous depths she saw swirling in his eyes. "If I do?" she asked.

He swept his arms open wide and smiled ferally. "Then I'm your man."

James could tell that Kirby was having second thoughts about their plan the minute they stepped into the boathouse owned by Mrs. Pendleton Barclay, the grande dame of Endicott, Indiana. The Regolith Regatta was about to get under way, Mrs. Barclay was about to pop the cork on a nice bottle of champagne and he and Kirby were about to officially launch Operation Man-Killer.

At least, he amended with a shake of his head, they would, as soon as Kirby took off her damned coat.

Although four days had passed since she'd conceded to let him act as her tour guide on their trip down Bad Reputation Avenue, the regatta was going to be their first real opportunity to put their plan into action. It had rained the day of the Parallax Parade, and—in addition to the grand marshal's float having deteriorated to naught but chicken wire in no time flat—no one had been able to appreciate Kirby's skimpy red outfit beneath her bright yellow rain slicker, her enormous yellow rain hat and her big, black galoshes.

Today was nowhere near cool, but that hadn't kept Kirby from insisting that she don a lightweight coat over the skintight, dangerously scooped-neck, skimpy little purple dress she was also— almost—wearing. But she wouldn't be able to protest much longer. Since Mrs. Barclay had invited them to watch the regatta from her boathouse, they could pass the time in relative comfort, no coat necessary.

Relative being the operative word here, James knew. Because where Kirby was concerned, he was wondering if he would ever feel comfortable again.

Boathouse, however, was actually a deceptive term, seeing as how their current surroundings could very well have been featured in *Southern Living* magazine. A small, two-story Victorian wonder, Mrs. Barclay's place on the river was awash in pastels and Ralph Lauren for the Home. Panoramic bay windows in all the front rooms meant a gush of sunlight, and an outstanding view of the Ohio River and the rolling green hills of Kentucky on the other side. Strategically placed bars and buffets throughout meant guests could wander freely anywhere in the house without fear of having refreshment more than a room away.

All in all, the boathouse was...homey. Warm. Inviting. And it infused him with a feeling of well-being. Odd, that, James thought, seeing as how the very thought of anything homey normally sent him into paroxysms of terror. Deciding not to dwell on the matter, he turned to Kirby, only to find that she was still wearing her coat. He rolled his eyes heavenward in a silent bid for patience.

"Can I take your coat?" he asked for perhaps the tenth time since they had left Kirby's house.

"No!" she cried yet again, clutching the garment fiercely in both hands.

He inhaled deeply, counted to ten and released the breath slowly. "Kirby," he began with all the leniency he could muster, "take off your coat. If this plan has a hope in hell of working, you're going to have to do it eventually, and it might as well be now."

But she only seized the coat more insistently in her hands and glared at him.

"Kirby..." He tried again.

Her grip on the coat lessened some, but she still looked anything but certain about what she was doing. "I think I've changed my mind," she said softly. "I think I don't want to do this after all. I think we should go home and just forget about it. In fact, I think—"

"Teddy Gundersen is here," James interrupted her.

Kirby whipped around at the announcement, following the direction he had indicated with his finger. There, on the other side of the room, speaking with the woman James had learned was the mayor of Endicott, was the illustrious Mr. Gundersen in all his blond, Nordic glory. James had to fight back the wave of nausea that overtook him when he glanced back at Kirby, and saw her blushing in that way he'd come to realize meant she was entertaining thoughts no trembling—or even steadfast—virgin should be entertaining.

Dammit, why couldn't she look at him with the same lusty, hungry look she was throwing Teddy's way? James wondered. He wasn't a bad-looking sort himself. He worked out regularly and took pains with his hygiene, and he dressed impeccably. He gazed down at his dark plum trousers and printed, short-sleeved sport shirt that had been featured in a *GQ* spread just last month, then took in Teddy's tight, faded Levi's and denim work shirt unbuttoned down to *there*. Talk about obvious wardrobe, he thought morosely.

"Oh, and look. Henry Monroe is here, too," he added when he spied another object of Kirby's affections.

"Where?" Her gaze whipped around again.

"And Mark Benedict, as well," he concluded as a cool lump of something very unpleasant settled in his belly. "Well, haven't we just struck the jackpot today?"

"Where?" Once more, she turned her attention to the direction James indicated.

"Now, then, you were saying?" he asked dryly. "About your coat?"

"Uh..."

Her fingers on the coat loosened a bit more, hovering around the top button. She turned back to look at James, and her blush deepened significantly. Boy, she must *really* be entertaining some lascivious thoughts about the men in the room, he marveled, wondering which one in particular had brought about her heightened color.

When her fingers slowly began to slip the button through its hole, he found that he simply could not look away. One by one, leisurely, uncertainly, she unfastened each of the buttons holding her coat closed. When the last one had been freed, she gripped each side of the garment in her hands and began to shrug it from her shoulders.

Good God, what was wrong with him? James wondered as he released a breath he'd been unaware of holding. He was suddenly feeling more turned on by watching a woman take off her coat than he'd ever been watching a woman remove her underthings. Somehow, the view of Kirby fully dressed, concealing instead of revealing, was a bigger turn-on for him than the sight of any other woman naked had been. Man, he really had it bad.

She skimmed the coat off completely and extended it to James, who took it from her graciously and, he hoped, without a single hint of the way his blood was stampeding through his veins. Then she stood before him—and everyone else in the room—dressed in the skintight, teeny-tiny clothing that showcased her long, long legs and round, round bottom better than Saran Wrap would have.

And then, as if her pheromones had just jumped right up and shouted, "Yahtzee!" every male eye in the room homed in to focus on the sight.

Teddy Gundersen halted his conversation with the mayor in midsentence, his mouth agape, his eyes afire.

Henry Monroe choked on the shrimp puff he'd just popped into his mouth, and began to cough erratically.

Mark Benedict dropped his beer with a crash and a splash to the floor.

And James gritted his teeth. Hard.

"I, uh...I think you've got their attention," he said.

"Kirby!" the three men chorused.

As one, they all exchanged wary glances with each other. Then, as they all seemed to remember themselves, they each began a not-so-leisurely stroll toward her, mayor, shrimp puff and spilled beer clearly forgotten. And miraculously, James noted, they all managed to avoid tripping over their tongues as they approached. Amazing.

As they drew nearer, he couldn't resist leaning forward to whisper in her ear, "Be gentle with them, Mata Hari. For they know not what awaits them." Then, not trusting himself to remain civil should any of those undeserving geeks so much as drool on the toe of one of her high-heeled pumps, he sauntered away with feigned indifference.

Unfortunately, he realized as he made his way forward, he had absolutely no idea where he was going. Although, when he thought about it, he decided it would probably be best if he had someone lock him in a closet for the duration of the regatta party. That way, he wouldn't have to watch a bunch of yahoos slobbering all over Kirby Connaught. That way, there would be no chance of his feeling compelled to thunder in like a paladin and sweep her into his arms, then ride off into the sunset with her. That way, he might have some vague chance of battling this sudden urge to cleave in two those black-hearted knights undeserving of such purity and goodness and light.

He shook his head incredulously at the imagery he had woven. Boy, since when had he become such a dragon-slayer? he wondered. Kirby was anything but a lady in distress. Weighing in at a cool one hundred and sixteen pounds, she was "Man-Killer" Connaught, he reminded himself. He knew she was, because he'd given her the proper lessons himself. And she'd more than bowled him over with that kiss the two of them had shared the other night.

What an *idiot,* he chastised himself now. What on earth had he been thinking to mine out the woman's erogenous potential and unleash it on any Teddy, Mark or Henry who came down the pike?

He spun around with every intention of rescuing her from the men's clutches—or, more accurately, rescuing them from hers—only to find her smiling shyly as each of the men extended a cup of punch toward her. Punch, James noted. Not wine, not champagne, not Johnnie Walker Black and water with a twist, which is what he had instructed her that any self-respecting woman of sophistication over the age of twenty-one would ask her date to bring her. No, Kirby had evidently put in a request for punch. Or else the men had simply taken it upon themselves to procure punch for her.

Punch, he marveled again. Something only an innocent would appreciate.

And that was when he realized that there was more to muddying a woman's reputation than dressing her in a short skirt and draping her on the arm of a rogue. Oh, certainly, the rogue date would raise eyebrows and the short skirt would attract ogles, but that inherent innocence inside Kirby was just way too deeply ingrained for any man to be overcome with the urge to, uh, soil her, by the simple sight of nice gams. James halted as he considered the scene.

Yes, Teddy, Mark and Henry were all interested. But they weren't yet eyeing her with that look all men recognized as blatant, unmitigated lust. They weren't making silly, little suggestive comments about her apparel. They weren't leaning in to get a better look at the dusky valley between her breasts that the tight dress did nothing to hide and everything to enhance. Instead, they all seemed to be blushing as profoundly as Kirby was.

James shook his head. What was it with this town? he wondered. Was no one morally bankrupt? Sheesh.

This called for drastic action. If James was going to ruin Kirby's reputation—and suddenly, he was more determined than ever to do just that—then he was going to have to act fast. For some reason, he forgot all about the fact that only a moment ago, he'd been wanting to rescue her from her suitors. Now, suddenly, he was intent on proving to the three men that the lady in question was in fact no lady at all, and that she was more than worthy of their unworthy attentions.

Or at least, worthy of his own unworthy attentions.

Marshaling every bad boy maneuver in his arsenal as grandly as he could, James quickly formed a strategy, squared his shoulders and entered into the fray.

Kirby was more than a little flustered, trying to fend off the attentions of three men at once, when she'd never been able to attract the attentions of even one before. And oddly enough, the realization that Teddy, Mark and Henry were all vying for her favors right now—something that as recently as a week ago would have been an impossible fantasy—made her feel anything but happy. Actually, as she watched the three men smiling and blushing, shuffling their feet and batting their eyelashes at her, what she was feeling was...kind of irritable.

Just who did they think they were? she wondered. Here she'd been trying for more than a year to attract their attention, and they'd all run screaming in the other direction. Now, suddenly, just because she put on a short, tight skirt and a little mascara—okay and some really, really red lipstick, too—they wanted to get to know her better. How superficial could they get?

Of course, she thought further, however reluctantly, there *was* another potential explanation for their sudden change of behavior, as much as she hated to dwell on it.

Bob.

That darned comet. It was drawing nearer and nearer to the earth with each passing hour, and was doubtless wreaking havoc on the senses of just about everyone in Endicott. It was common knowledge that Bob delighted in messing with people's heads, and nothing could be more evident lately than the fact that the comet was doing just that. Everywhere she looked in town, people were acting strangely.

Mrs. Winslow, the librarian, was lusting after Keanu Reeves. Angie's father had invited a mobster to dinner. Rosemary had been dropping hints that she was actually beginning to *like* Willis Random. Men were starting to look at Kirby as if they were wondering what she had on beneath her dress. If anything.

And Kirby had begun to wonder if maybe she herself wasn't as big a victim of Bob's as anyone. What else could explain her overriding fascination with James Nash? What other reason could there be for her daydreams that pictured her and James not just writhing naked and tangled amid her sheets—which was certainly disturbing enough to visualize—but living in her mother's house, surrounded by a half-dozen children, some with gray eyes, some with blue, half of them blond and the other half ebony-haired?

It must be the comet, she reasoned. What else could it be? Surely she could just blame it on Bob, right?

And it was just as likely that Teddy, Mark and Henry were all similarly succumbing to the comet. There was every chance that the three men were simply lusting after her—because they were clearly lusting after her—due to a cosmic influence they couldn't fight. Bob was doubtless playing mind games with them, too, and that was the *only* reason they'd all taken a sudden, obviously more than brotherly, interest in her.

Or, she conceded with a sigh, maybe it was just the short, tight dress and really red lipstick.

Again she found herself wondering what had possessed her to think this was a good idea. Then, as if the thought had conjured him up, she looked past Teddy and saw James approaching. And he had a look of determination in his eyes that she didn't like one bit.

"Here you go, Kirby, darling," he called out when he was still a good ten feet away.

Darling?

She was so surprised by his use of the endearment that she actually glanced over her shoulder to see if someone else named Kirby had shown up behind her. But when all she saw was the wall, she turned her puzzled gaze back to James.

"Um, yes...dear?" she asked, hoping she was supposed to be playing along with whatever game he had started.

He held a drink in each hand, and thrust one of them toward her—a glass that appeared to hold ice water. She took it from him automatically, still trying to figure out what he was up to.

"Well, my, my, my," James said mildly, eyeing each of the other men in turn. He offered Kirby a playfully chastising look.

"I leave your side for one minute to get you a drink, and what happens? All these local boys move in on my territory. And here I thought you midwesterners respected each other's right to own property. All that farming stuff that goes back generations."

Right to own property? Kirby thought. He was calling her his *property?* Just what did James think he was doing? She noted that each of the other men eyed him back warily, though none seemed quite willing to challenge his right to claim her as acreage. Not yet, at any rate.

"James..." she began, hoping the warning came through loud and clear.

"Well, no matter," he said as he elbowed his way between Teddy and Henry and took up a proprietary place by her side. He looped his arm around her waist and pulled her close. "Go on, sweetheart, drink up," he told her, still watching the other men. "I know how you like to put that stuff away. God knows I wouldn't want to come between you and your...refreshment."

Still confused by what he was saying—or, rather, by what he was not saying—Kirby gripped the glass firmly in her hands, thankful for something to hold on to that wasn't a body part of James Nash. Because having him standing so close roused instincts she'd just as soon not be feeling in a public place.

So she curled the fingers of both hands around her glass and lifted it to her lips. But she was only half paying attention as she drank, so focused was she on trying to figure out where James's fingers seemed to be creeping—namely down to her fanny. After filling her mouth with the cool, clear liquid, she swallowed, then immediately began to cough. Or rather, hack. Loudly.

"I'm sorry," James said apologetically when he noted her distress. He patted her helpfully on the back. "I should have warned you it wasn't what you usually drink. I know you like tequila straight up, but they have an inferior brand at the bar, so I had them pour you gin instead. A double," he added casually, "since you drink like a fish."

Kirby wanted to demand what the heck he thought he was talking about, but the fire that had begun in her throat suddenly trailed down her esophagus, past her heart, and raged to life in her belly. James patted her back a bit more insistently, urging the glass back up to her mouth.

"Have another sip," he told her. "If you still don't like it, I'll have the bartender run out for a bottle of Cuervo and a shaker of salt. That is, after all, your habitual manner of consumption, isn't it?"

"I..." Another round of hacking prevented Kirby from completing her objection. So James urged the glass back up to her mouth in silent encouragement. The last thing she wanted to do was ingest another mouthful of that drain cleaner, so she shook her head adamantly in refusal.

James sighed petulantly. "All right, all right. I know what a spitting, vicious little alley cat you become when you can't have your way."

He pulled her close and dipped his head to her neck, then bestowed a big, slurpy kiss on her collarbone. Before Kirby had the chance to object, he pulled back some and added with a purr of delight, "And although I can't even begin to describe how much that turns me on when we're alone, it's nothing we need to unleash on the unsuspecting public, is it? Cuervo it is. Boys?" he asked further as he turned to their other companions. "I can trust you to keep your mitts off her while I'm gone, can't I?"

Even through the tears that still stung her eyes, Kirby could see the other three men nod their heads in unified, albeit mystified, agreement. And all she could think then was that it was going to indeed bring her great delight to be alone with James later—when she could tear him limb from limb with her bare hands. A spitting, vicious little alley cat, huh? He hadn't seen nothin' yet.

Unfortunately, she wasn't going to be able to throttle him until later. For now, she had little choice but to play along with whatever bizarre plan he had in mind, because she had no idea how to counteract with one of her own. At the moment, every eye in the room was on her, watching, waiting to see how she would react to James's obvious stake of claim, not to mention the aspersions he had just cast on her character. Be cool, she told herself. The last thing she wanted to do was create a scene.

After all, her reputation was at stake.

* * *

The Regolith Regatta party at Mrs. Barclay's wound up being an exercise in complete futility. As did the Castor and Pollux Two-Legged Race the following day. And the Triton Tug-O-War that followed two days after that.

They were *all* exercises in futility, Kirby reflected now, as she stood before the mirror in the girls' rest room of her high school alma mater, marveling again at the latest outfit of James's selection. Because for every single event, she'd been dressed up and shown off like a prize pig at the fair, and always, James Nash had been the one holding proudly on to her leash, refusing to surrender it to anyone.

Worse than that, however, had been his behavior. Or, more accurately, his *mis*behavior. Everywhere they'd gone together, he'd made clear to anyone who would listen that he and Kirby were all but joined at the hip. Or worse, joined in other places that people traditionally only joined together when they were trying to propagate the species.

He had made it a point to keep her right by his side at all times, and to accomplish that, he had always had an arm roped possessively around her waist. Or looped around her neck. Or linked through her elbow. Or else he'd have a hand splayed open at the small of her back. Or cupped over her shoulder. Or cradling her fanny.

She squeezed her eyes shut as she recalled some of the ways James had touched her over the last week. And although she told herself she should completely resent being paraded around as a prized possession of that promiscuous playboy Peeping Tom, a part of her had to admit she'd enjoyed it.

It had been fun, being a bad girl for a change, even if it was all an act. She *liked* seeing the raised eyebrows of the social and moral bastions of Endicott. She *liked* having men like Teddy and Henry and Mark gaping at her with their tongues lolling out of their mouths like spaniels'. She *liked* knowing she was burning up the rumor mill for reasons other than her numerous good deeds for the day. It had felt good to strip off the mantle of innocence and purity and cloak herself in the skimpy attire of hot stuff for a change. Even if it was only temporary. And even if it was all in jest.

Unfortunately, though, all good things had to come to an end. Because as much fun as she'd been having as a fallen woman, deep down, Kirby knew it was all just an act. She was still a virgin. She still blushed at the suggestion of impropriety. She still wasn't comfortable in the revealing attire she'd adopted. She wasn't really the siren Endicott seemed to think she had become. And she certainly wasn't the object of James Nash's uncontrollable libido, nor the receptacle for his incessant sexual drive.

As much as she might wish that she was.

But she still had one more week to pretend, she reminded herself. One more week before the festival ended and James was on his way to destinations far more exotic than Endicott, Indiana. One more week to play the part of the fallen innocent whose purity would be forever stained by the dark lover who had seduced her. One more week to delude herself that he might eventually fall in love with her. One more week to delude herself that she hadn't fallen in love with him.

One more week. It seemed like no time at all and more than an eternity. But for what exactly, she had no idea.

So tonight, she was going to make the most of it. Tonight was the night for the traditional Comet Stomp Dance at the high school, and Kirby and James had signed on as chaperones. Although now that she got another look at herself in the mirror, she wondered if it was actually legal for her to turn out dressed as she was in front of a gymnasium full of minors.

The little black cocktail dress was long on little and short on dress, with black spaghetti straps, a plunging neckline, an even more plunging back and a hemline that fell just short of her...well, never mind. She could already hear the phone at church ringing off the hook when the parents of her Sunday school students found out that Jezebel herself was offering up Bible lessons that were best left in the home. Pushing the thought away, Kirby dragged a brush quickly through her hair, touched up her lipstick and headed for the door.

Outside, leaning carelessly against the wall waiting for her, was James. Dressed in black trousers, another collarless shirt—this one in emerald green—with his hair pulled back in his ponytail, he looked like a high-priced model. Kirby still couldn't quite get over how handsome he was, how sexy, how sophisticated. And she still couldn't quite figure out why, with all the available women in Endicott, when she was clearly nothing at all that he needed or desired in a woman, he was still hanging around with her.

Bob.

The word leapt into her brain with the force of a falling meteor. That was the only explanation that made any sense. The comet must be messing with James the same way it was messing with everyone else in town. This was the weekend Bob would make his closest approach to the planet, when fifteen-year-olds who'd been infants the last time he'd made an appearance would all be gazing skyward and uttering wishes to be fulfilled fifteen years hence. It was a time for magic. And somehow, Kirby knew she wouldn't be disappointed.

For a moment, she thought back to the night when she was fifteen herself, when she and Angie and Rosemary had all lain in the cool clover at the very darkest corner of Angie's backyard, and watched as a hazy little speck in the sky twinkled down upon them.

A forever-after kind of love, she recalled with a sigh, taking in the sight of James in all his elegant, worldly glory. And as he pushed himself away from the wall, as he shoved his hands into his pants pockets and sauntered casually toward her, as he unleashed that sexy, toe-curling smile on her, she realized in a flash of understanding something that hadn't occurred to her before.

Bob had granted her wish, after all. Because in that moment, Kirby knew she was in love with James Nash. Totally, irrevocably. A forever-after kind of love that would stay with her until the day she died.

Eight

Kirby wasn't sure when it had happened, or how, but she was as certain of it now as she was her own name. She did love James, and probably had since that moment in the library when he'd touched her so gently, so tenderly...so differently from any other man.

He was going to be the one who was the grand passion in her lifetime. He would be the one she would never forget, the one whose face would rise up out of nowhere to haunt her when she least expected it, the one whose voice, whose scent, whose feel would jar her out of a deep sleep for scores of nights to come.

She would love James forever after. She knew that with all her heart. Bob had granted her wish. Why then was she so unhappy?

Because it was supposed to have been a two-way street, she answered herself immediately. The man she loved was supposed to love her back. She remembered now that she hadn't exactly made that part of her wish as specific as she probably could have. But surely Bob would have understood. Surely he would have realized how painful it was to love someone who didn't love you in return. Surely he wouldn't be so merciless as to play a joke of such cosmic proportions on someone who didn't deserve it.

Surely.

"Ready to go in?" James asked her as he halted in front of her. "Ready to play the game?"

The game. That was how the two of them had begun to refer to Operation Man-Killer. It was a game, she supposed, because they were playing for stakes. But games were supposed to be fun, weren't they? she thought. And it occurred to her then that she wasn't having nearly as much as she could be having.

And suddenly, to Kirby, it wasn't a game anymore at all.

"I'm ready to go in," she said, sidestepping the other part of his question. "But only if you promise me at least one dance."

"Only one?" he asked, clearly surprised. "Sweetheart, I don't intend to let you out of my sight for the entire evening. You're going to break hearts in that dress."

Well, maybe some hearts, she thought. But not the one that counted.

"Break hearts?" she echoed. "I thought I was supposed to be collecting them."

At her softly uttered comment, his expression grew shuttered, and Kirby couldn't understand why. "Well, yeah," he said, stumbling a bit over the words. "Of course you're supposed to be collecting them. That's what I meant."

She studied him for a moment, then asked, "If the whole point to Operation Man-Killer is to round up a group of likely suitors for me, then how come every time a man comes close, you move in and claim me for yourself?"

James eyed Kirby back with a speculation to rival her own, but he didn't respond right away. Her question was a valid one, and it deserved an equally valid answer. Unfortunately, he was fresh out of answers at the moment, because all he had swirling around in his brain lately were questions. Lots of questions.

Like how come he suddenly didn't want Operation Man-Killer to succeed? Like why did it bother him so much to see the very men they were trying to lure into Kirby's bed falling at her feet every time she went out anywhere dressed in her Man-Killer costume? Like what was the point of continuing with this whole farce when *he* wanted to be the man lured into her bed? Like what the hell he thought he was thinking wanting to stay in her bed with her forever?

Because that's exactly what had been happening. The more time he'd spent with Kirby, the more time he wanted. That first day he'd made her acquaintance, his intentions for her had been nothing more than temporary. He'd planned on staying in Endicott for three weeks. And he'd figured in three weeks' time, he'd have about as much of Kirby Connaught as he could stand.

Of course, at the time, he'd figured it would only be a matter of hours before he had her in his bed—or found himself in hers—but that was beside the point. The point was that he, James Nash, globe-trotter, pop icon, debauchee, Most Desirable Man in America, promiscuous playboy Peeping Tom, had developed a big ol' crush on Kirby Connaught, virgin, midwesterner, teetotaler, Sunday school teacher, nice kid.

He'd never had a crush on anyone before. And frankly, he wasn't sure how to act. So he fell back on an old trick, one that had never failed to work for him before. He refused to think about it.

"James?"

However, the sound of his name, uttered with such focus and longing, brought his attention back to the matter at hand. And he realized then that Kirby was going to make him think about it, whether he liked it or not. "What?"

"Why have you been keeping every man who shows an interest in me at arm's length?" she asked again.

Oh, yeah. That. "Um..." he began eloquently. "It's because, ah... Well, you see..."

But try as he might to answer the question, he realized he simply could not. So what did Kirby do? She asked him another one.

"Because wasn't the whole point to this thing to find a man who would fall in love with me forever-after?" she began again, evidently unwilling to let it go until he gave her an explanation for his behavior.

Gee, he really wished he had one to offer her. Or to himself, for that matter. Unfortunately, like answers, he was fresh out of explanations lately, too. So he turned an ear to the faraway sound of a band playing, and seized on that instead. "Do you hear that?" he asked, taking her hand in his. "They're playing one of my favorite songs." He tugged lightly on her fingers. "Come on. Dance with me."

She seemed reluctant to follow him, and for a moment he feared she would dig in and refuse to go anywhere until he had offered her a sufficient answer to her question. He held his breath as five seconds passed...then ten...then more... At last, she appeared willing to drop the subject, because she smiled at him and took a cautious step forward.

But there was something about her smile that bothered James. It wasn't a happy smile, he realized. It was a smile of resolution and acceptance, the kind of smile a person might smile, knowing a painful experience was finally over.

Odd, that sad smile, he thought. What could she possibly have to feel sad about? Nearly everyone in Endicott was talking about her these days, and not in the way they had been before. James knew this to be a fact, because he had sent Begley out snooping to the Dew Drop Inn and Dot's Donut Hut. And the valet—once he'd finished waxing poetic over the delectable Jewel—had reported back that nearly every available man in town was marveling at the changes that had come over their sweet, innocent, virginal little Kirby Connaught.

Better than that, however, they were all speculating over whether the changes were the result of natural or unnatural causes.

The natural cause, of course, would be Bob. Theories were rampant that, just as the comet was wreaking havoc with so many other people in town, Bob was obviously inflicting his cosmic mayhem on Kirby, too, making her say and do and wear things she would normally *never* say or do or wear. It must be Bob, the townsfolk were saying. Because if it wasn't, then it must be that other, unnatural cause. That unnatural cause being, James recalled with more than a touch of pride, none other than James Nash.

Either way, Kirby's virtue had definitely fallen prey to much supposition. Was she, or wasn't she? Had she, or hadn't she? No one seemed to know for sure, but everyone seemed eager to find out. All that was left now was for one of the local lads to step in after James was gone and pick up the pieces he left behind.

Six months. Twelve at the max. That's how long he figured it would be before Kirby marched down the aisle, resplendent in wedding finery, on the arm of a besotted local boy who would never know what had hit him.

And that, James realized much to his own shock, was something he just didn't want to think about. So he gazed at Kirby again, absorbed the clarity of her blue eyes, the shimmer of her white-blond hair, the softly sculpted features of her face.

Little by little, he drank in everything about her, and all he could do was repeat softly, "Dance with me."

Her response was another step forward, followed by another, and then another. Within moments, they had made their way to the edge of the crowd dancing in the high school gymnasium. They hid themselves amid a circle of darkness, their bodies pressed together close, their foreheads touching. And they swayed languidly to a tune of their own making, because the one the band played commanded much more exertion than either was willing to expend.

Kirby didn't know if anyone had seen them enter together, or if anyone was watching them now. And even though that was the whole point to this endeavor, at the moment she didn't care. All she knew was that James was here, he was close and he was hers. At least for tonight. And, if her luck held out and Bob was smiling on her, perhaps for a week full of nights to come. And she decided then that she would do her best to make the most of it.

Maybe James wouldn't love her forever after, she conceded. But maybe Bob would be generous enough to give him to her for a week.

They were so perfectly in tune, she marveled as they danced. Their bodies seemed to respond to each other instinctively. Whenever James moved, her body moved with him. And whenever she changed the tempo or the direction, he automatically followed her. Poetry in motion, she thought with a smile. Not bad for a couple of people with tarnished reputations.

He took another step forward, wrapping his arms around her waist, pulling her as close to himself as he could. Against her belly, she felt him swelling to life and knew that he was as affected by the motion of their bodies as she was. Although they were dancing near a door that had been pushed open wide to allow in the cool September evening, she was quickly growing hot. His heat surrounded her, mingling with her own, driving the temperature to combustible levels. And she knew then that spontaneously combusting with James was going to be unavoidable.

So she, too, took a step forward and wound her arms around his back. Then, feeling more daring and dangerous than ever, she shifted her pelvis to drag her midsection against his. Back and forth, back and forth. And like a girl with a bad reputation, she delighted in the gasp of pleasure he expelled in response. Even better was the rumble of delight that followed, a sound that seemed to bubble up from the deepest, darkest recesses of his soul.

"Kirby..." he whispered, the danger signals in his voice unmistakable.

But instead of heeding his warning, she only shimmied her body against his again, and skimmed the hands on his back lower, down to his waist, to his hips.

"Kirby..." he repeated, his cautious tone this time punctuated by a strangled little sound.

"Hmm?" she murmured as she moved her hands again. She scooped them low to cup his taut buttocks in her palms, briefly, but with much affection, before brushing her fingers back up to his waist again.

"Oh, Kirby..."

Her heart began to pound rapid-fire at the sound of utter longing in his voice. He sounded almost as desperate as she felt.

"Yes, James?" she asked, surprised that she was able to feign a calmness she was nowhere near feeling.

"You, uh...you want to tell me what you think you're doing?"

She pulled back far enough to glance up at his face. Then she smiled what she hoped was the smile of a woman who was up to no good. "I was squeezing your butt," she told him frankly, fighting back a laugh at the shocked expression that crossed his face. She batted her eyelashes like a coquette. "I'm sorry. Didn't

I do it right? I'm kind of new at this, having never squeezed a man's butt before.''

He chuckled, a low, long sound of delight. "Then maybe you should do it again, just to be sure.''

She smiled once more, curling her fingers into the warm, solid flesh of his back, reveling in the heat that seeped through his shirt and into her fingertips. Then, oh so slowly, she dragged her hands downward, lingering for a moment at his waist before dipping lower still. She covered his fanny with both hands, pressed her fingers into the curve of each buttock and urged his body closer to her own.

"Oh, yeah," he whispered on a rush of air. "You did it just fine. Gee, I never would have guessed that was your first time.''

"Well, I have to confess—someone's been coaching me.''

He smiled back at her with much satisfaction. Then he began to dance her backward, away from the crowd, toward the open door that led into the sultry September night and welcome escape. Kirby had no idea where he intended to take her, but she couldn't wait to get there. Step by step, sway by sway, they continued, even after the music stopped. By the time the dim, multicolored lights in the gym began to flash bright white for a faster number from the band, she and James had passed through the door and into the night, under the welcome cover of darkness—utterly, blissfully alone.

James slammed the door behind them, checked to be sure it was locked and fixed her gaze with his. Then he spun her around and pressed her against the side of the gymnasium, the cool, smooth concrete of the wall a welcome balm to the heated skin of her back and shoulders. He braced a forearm on the bricks above her head, flattened his palm over the wall beside her neck and covered her body with his.

And then he kissed her. Slowly. Hungrily. Thoroughly. His mouth possessed hers and she opened to him at once, inviting him inside, tasting him as deeply as he tasted her. Again and again he slanted his mouth across hers to enter her from another angle, seemingly unable to slake his thirst for her. All Kirby could do was grip his shirt in both fists and hold on tight for the ride.

She felt him everywhere—from the fingers that tangled leisurely in her hair to the hungry mouth tugging at hers, to the broad chest pressing against her tender breasts, to the hips he rotated against her belly. And everywhere he touched her, she was on fire. Never had she experienced such heat, such power, such a simmering just beneath her skin. James set a match to her heart, and the flame that ignited there spread to every cell in her body.

He insinuated his leg between hers and nudged them apart, and she gasped at the sensation that rippled through her at such an intimate caress. When he pushed his thigh against the heated core of her, her heart hammered rapid-fire. She cried out at the invasion of his strong muscles rubbing against so sensitive a part of her, and when she did, James dipped his head to her neck, dragging openmouthed kisses along her throat, her collarbone, her shoulder.

He dropped a hand to her hip and held her fast as he shifted his leg upward again. Instinctively she jerked forward to meet his thrust, the long, hard length of him driving her to near madness. His fingers at the hem of her dress dipped below the fabric, dragging it higher and higher over her bare leg, stopping only when he could shove his fingers under the lacy leg of her panties. Then he cupped his warm palm over the back of her thigh and urged it upward, moving his leg again, more insistently this time. She bucked against him, once, twice, three times, awed by the waves of pleasure crashing through her.

"Oh…" Kirby groaned. "Oh…please… Oh…*James*…"

"Tell me what you want, Kirby." His voice was as rough as hers was, his heartbeat raging in time with hers.

"You," she managed to whisper, uncertain exactly when she'd made the decision, knowing only that it was the right one. "I want you."

He bent his head to her neck again and brushed his lips against her throat with a series of quick, butterfly-soft kisses, completely at odds with the hand fiercely gripping her thigh and the demanding back-and-forth of his leg against her. "You want me to what?" he asked quietly.

"I…I want you…to…"

But he moved again, releasing her thigh and lowering it slowly.

Then he skimmed his fingers upward again, strumming them lightly up over her hip, her waist, her rib cage, halting to frame the lower curve of her breast with his thumb and forefinger. Kirby leaned into him, unconsciously urging him to complete the journey he'd undertaken. But James only rubbed his jaw over the crown of her head, inhaled deeply and continued to lovingly cradle her breast.

She held her own breath as she waited to see if he would go any further. And when he seemed to be waiting for a signal from her, she covered his hand with hers and moved them both up over her breast. With her palm pressed to the back of his hand, she silently commanded him to plunder at will, marveling at her own wantonness. But all he did was fill his hand with her, gently cupping her swollen flesh.

"You want me to...?" he asked.

How could he be so cool and collected? she wondered. And why did he insist she spell out for him what he already knew she was asking him to do? Wasn't it obvious? Was she really so innocent that she wasn't making her wishes known?

Somehow she managed to summon enough strength to tilt her head back and meet his gaze. And what she saw in his eyes nearly stopped her heart.

White-hot heat. Raw hunger. Unbridled power. Kirby wondered yet again what she thought she was doing, playing games like this with a man like him. Then she reminded herself that it wasn't a game. Not anymore. She was playing for keeps. Even if James wouldn't.

She inhaled deeply and held the breath inside until her heart rate began to slow down. Then she forced herself to smile, hoping she looked a lot more confident than she felt. "I want you to make good on your promise," she told him. "I want you to ruin my reputation."

He smiled back, flicking his thumb lightly over the erect peak of her breast. Kirby moaned, spirals of delight fluttering through her every time he moved his fingers against her. And all she could think was that she never, ever, wanted to stop feeling the way she felt then.

"Hey," he said softly, pulling her attention reluctantly back to their conversation, "in case you hadn't noticed, we've already halfway achieved that. As far as the good people of Endicott are concerned, your reputation is definitely in question these days."

She nodded. "Well, why keep everyone wondering?" she asked. "Why not let them know definitely? Since we're halfway there already, why not go all the way?"

He eyed her thoughtfully for a moment, as if he were weighing heavily in his mind what she had just said. She couldn't understand what he had to consider so seriously. As far as Kirby was concerned, what was happening between them now, what would doubtless occur as a result, was as unavoidable as the sunrise tomorrow morning.

But still James pondered in silence. Then, just when she thought he was going to turn her down, he murmured, "You sure you know what you're asking?"

She answered quickly and unequivocally. "Yes."

"You'll be giving away something you've prized and protected for thirty years," he pointed out.

"I know."

"And not to some local boy who'll build a white picket fence around that little pink house of yours, either."

"I know that, too."

"You'll be giving it to me. James Nash."

"Yes."

"That...what is it you keep calling me?"

"That promiscuous playboy Peeping Tom."

"Right. You'll be giving it to him instead."

"Yes."

He continued to meet her gaze levelly, his voice empty of any kind of emotion. "World traveler, international bad boy," he clarified further.

"Yes," she stated without concern.

"A man not worthy of the gift you're giving him in any way, shape or form."

She chose not to respond to that and remained silent instead, holding his gaze steady in a wordless invitation.

"I can't give you that forever-after kind of love you want, Kirby," he said, clearly wanting to make sure she knew what she was getting herself into. His eyes had grown dark and distant as he said it, as if he'd had to withdraw into himself to remind himself of the kind of man he really was.

And a little part of her died inside to realize that he was telling her the truth.

She wanted to reply that that was okay, that she had enough forever-after love in her own heart to last them both a lifetime and beyond. But she knew if she told him that, if she revealed how much he'd come to mean to her, then she'd be chasing him away faster than she'd scared off the local boys. So she held herself in check, hoped that somewhere inside his soul he understood somehow exactly what this meant to her and waited to see what he would do.

"Did you hear me?" he asked quietly. The hand on her breast skimmed upward, along her collarbone, over the column of her throat, to gently cup her jaw. Then he stroked his thumb tenderly over her cheekbone. "I can't love you, Kirby. Not any longer than tonight, or this week. Or maybe next week, if I'm lucky. I'm just not built that way."

She swallowed hard, but didn't flinch from his steady gaze. "I know that."

"And it doesn't matter to you?"

She didn't know how to answer that. Not really. Finally she told him, "Not tonight, it doesn't. And it won't this week. Or even next week, either."

He nodded silently, but seemed no more content with her answer than she was herself. In spite of that, he smiled. It was a quick, uneasy smile, but a smile nonetheless. And that was good enough for Kirby. She knew it was going to have to be.

With one final caress of her cheek, he stepped away from her, lacing her fingers with his, tugging her away from the wall. "Your place or mine, then?" he asked.

"Your place," she decided quickly. *That way there won't be as many memories haunting me after you've gone.*

He nodded slowly, then extended his hand to the right. "Okay, then. Let's do it."

She bit her tongue to keep from adding what she wanted to add, something about the two of them making wishes come true.

Because that was only half-right, she knew. Oh, yes, Bob had granted her wish for a forever-after kind of love. She only wondered now why she hadn't had the foresight fifteen years ago to ask that that love be returned. Too late now, she thought.

Nevertheless, she couldn't avoid glancing quickly up at the sky, searching for a tiny speck of light to the left of the moon and amending the request she had made fifteen years ago.

Nine

It was all James could do to keep his hands to himself as Omar drove them back to the Admiralty Inn. But making love while the chauffeur watched had never been one of his big fantasies, and he was fairly certain Kirby didn't want an audience for her first time. Especially since she was sitting beside him in that unbelievably sexy dress with her hands folded primly in her lap, smelling faintly of lavender, looking everywhere but at him.

Outside the car window beyond her, Endicott, Indiana, passed by him in a blur of oak trees and stucco houses, sidewalks and porch lamps, bicycles and minivans. Even when they neared downtown—*downtown,* he repeated to himself with a faint smile—he was greeted by the sight of squat brick buildings, white frame churches, mom-and-pop storefronts and the occasional neon sign.

This place was like none he had ever visited before, a slice of Middle America somehow left untainted by modern times. It was a place of innocence, a place of goodness, a place of decency. An oasis of escape from a planet going slowly mad, where wishes

wished by fifteen-year-old girls staring hopefully into the sky
were rumored to come true.

And Kirby Connaught belonged here.

The realization brought with it a profound shudder, though
whether one of heat or of cold James couldn't be certain. He only
knew that at that moment he could allow nothing to exist outside
the cocoon he and Kirby had created together. Whatever was
going to happen between them had been coming since the moment he'd gazed upon her through the lens of his telescope. It
felt preordained, inescapable. And he wanted nothing to interfere
with that.

But he'd never deflowered a virgin before. That realization
above all others kept circling in his head. He didn't want to hurt
her, didn't want her to look back on her first time with a fleeting
feeling of disappointment. He wanted her memories of him to be
filled with pleasure and fondness. Fifty years from now, he
wanted Kirby to be an old woman sitting in a porch swing with
a wistful smile on her face as she looked back on those wild
weeks she spent with the man who had been her first.

But he had no idea what to do to make sure he didn't hurt her.
To make sure she experienced a deep, prolonged ecstasy like none
she'd ever known. He'd never been anyone's first time before.
And then another thought struck him, with the force of two worlds
that collide.

In that sense, this was going to be a first time for him, too.

Yet, instead of bothering him, the realization soothed the trou-
bled ripple of his thoughts. He would be Kirby's first lover. She
would be his first innocent. Somehow that made all the difference
in the world. Somehow, suddenly, the odds seemed much more
workable.

When he turned to look at her, he found her gazing straight
ahead. So he lifted a hand to her face and brushed his fingertips
lightly along the elegant line of her jaw. She started when he did
so, jerking her head around to look at him. She was scared, he
saw, something that brought him more comfort. Because why
should he be the only one who was frightened about what lay
ahead?

"What are you thinking about?" he asked her softly.

She dipped her head, dropping her gaze to the fingers twined nervously together in her lap. "I'll give you three guesses," she told him with a soft smile.

He feigned consideration. "Could it be the stability of the global marketplace?" he asked.

She shook her head, her smile broadening.

"Hmm..." He began again. "Then it must be whether or not the Colts have a snowball's chance of making the Super Bowl this year."

She shook her head and quietly chuckled. "No. Not that, either."

"Well, then. It could only be one other thing."

When he said nothing further, she brought her head back up to look at him. He was relieved to see not fear now, but humor sparkling in her eyes, and was oddly pleased to know that he was the source of it. She arched her eyebrows at him in silent query.

"If you're not concerned about the state of the global marketplace," he said, "and if you're not worried about the Colts, then there could only be one other thing that has your thoughts so clearly bound up with a pink satin bow."

Again she only gazed at him in silent question.

"Me," he said simply.

She smiled, nodded and ducked her head down again.

"Anything in particular weighing heavily on your mind?" he asked further. He just wanted her to talk, to say something—anything—so he would know for sure that she wasn't just a vision he had conjured up from his fantasies through so intense a longing.

"Oh, one or two things," she conceded.

He was about to ask her if she could be more specific, but the car rolled to a halt in front of the Admiralty Inn, bringing a similar halt to their conversation. Omar unfolded his big body from behind the wheel and strode easily around the front of the car, then opened Kirby's door and extended a hand to help her out. The hotel doorman snapped to attention at the sight of them before reaching for the door and pulling it open wide.

As always, and without even thinking about what he was doing, James offered both his driver and the doorman a brief, meaningless smile, dropped his hand to the small of Kirby's back and escorted her inside. It was a scene he'd played out in his life a thousand different times, in a thousand different places, with a thousand different women. But never before had he felt the flutter of butterflies dancing about in his belly. Never had his pulse hammered so erratically. Never had he felt as if he were half in love with the woman by his side.

First time, he thought again, the words echoing over and over.

Neither of them said a word as they rode the elevator to the twelfth floor, nor as they strode down the hall to his suite, nor as James inserted the key into the lock and gave it a gentle twist. The room was quiet and softly lit when they entered it, the bed already turned down by housekeeping, two little foil-wrapped chocolate hearts having been left on one of the pillows. He started to close the door, then noticed the Do Not Disturb sign hanging on the inside knob. He hooked it on the outside, closed the door gently and locked it behind them.

When he turned around, he saw Kirby standing in the middle of the room, staring at the bed as if it were a fire-breathing dragon. So he moved slowly up behind her, dropped his hands lightly over her shoulders and leaned in close.

"Are you sure this is what you want?" he asked her, holding his breath as he awaited her reply.

"Yes," she said immediately, without a hint of uncertainty. She spun around and spread her hands open on his chest, then skimmed them up over his shoulders and around his neck. "I've never been more sure of anything in my life," she told him. "This feels so... I can't describe it. Just...right. It feels right. It feels like this is exactly what's supposed to be happening. Does that make any sense at all?"

He nodded. "Yeah, it does."

She nodded back, then linked her fingers at his nape and took a step closer to him, close enough that he could feel her heat, could fill his lungs with the scent of her. Instinctively he settled his hands on her waist, rubbing his thumbs lightly over the silky fabric of her dress. And he remembered that beneath it, her skin was even softer. But he said nothing, made no other move than that, waiting for some indication from her that he should proceed.

"Well?" she finally asked, the hint of a smile dancing about her lips.

He arched his eyebrows in question, uncertain what she wanted him to say. "Well...what?"

She lifted one shoulder and let it drop in what he supposed was meant to be a shrug. Then she took another step closer, touching her body to his, tangling her fingers in the ponytail at his nape, sending a shiver of delight down to his very core. She propelled herself up on her tiptoes and brought her mouth to within an inch of his own.

And softly, very softly, she said, "So what are you waiting for?"

He couldn't help but smile at that. He slid his hands down over her hips, to the backs of her thighs, then up over her bottom. He wasn't sure, but he thought she uttered a quiet sound of arousal, or perhaps contentment, as his fingers splayed open over the soft curves beneath her dress.

"What am *I* waiting for?" he asked.

She nodded, but said nothing more.

"I guess I'm waiting for you to let me know how you want this thing to go."

"How should I know how it's supposed to go?" she asked, her voice a quiet purr. "I've never done this before. I thought you were supposed to be the expert."

He shook his head resolutely and pulled her a little closer. "Not with you, sweetheart. With you, I'm as green as they come."

She smiled at that, and he could see that she thought he was joking. It was just as well she didn't know he was telling her the truth, he told himself. There was no reason she needed to know this was the first time for both of them. Especially since she obviously took some comfort thinking one of them knew what they were doing.

Whatever.

She was watching him closely, clearly willing to defer to him in this matter of lovemaking that she knew nothing about. James had to tamp down the rising tide of desire that swelled to life inside him at her easy acquiescence. She trusted him, he marveled. Trusted him to initiate her tenderly. Trusted him not to disappoint her. Trusted him to make her first time memorable.

Go slow, he commanded himself. *Take your time. You've got all night. All night. All night...*

Then James, too, relinquished control, and surrendered to whatever it was that had brought him and Kirby together. He bent his head to hers and covered her mouth with his own.

And felt a fireball burst to life inside him.

She met him more than halfway, returning his kiss with a hunger and need to rival his own. Her response to him was instinctive—earthy, primitive, basic. He was a man. She was a woman. Anything that had come before was immaterial. Anything that would occur hence was of no import. Right here, right now, Kirby was all that he needed or wanted. And he hoped like hell he would be enough for her.

And then he ceased to think at all, because she wound her fingers in the ponytail at his nape and freed the band holding it. His hair rushed forward, over his shoulders, enveloping them both until she drove her hands deep into it and pushed it back again. She framed his face with her palms and turned her head to the side, then kissed him more deeply still.

Kirby couldn't imagine what had come over her to make her act so boldly and take such initiative with James. She only knew that suddenly she wanted nothing more in the world than to be united with him—physically, emotionally, spiritually—and she would do whatever it took to achieve that. Her breathing became thready and quick at the feel of his mouth on hers, and suddenly she couldn't get close enough to him.

So she crowded herself into his big body as he returned her kiss. And she sighed against his mouth when he drew his hands up from her hips, over her back, until his fingers found the place where her dress ended and her bare skin began. For a moment she felt his fingertips dancing across her heated flesh, as if he were trying to imprint the feel of her upon himself. Then his thumb tripped over the tongue of her zipper, and without hesitation, with a whisper of sound, he began to draw the fastening down.

Instinctively she went still in his arms, and immediately he halted the motion of his hand. He pulled his mouth from hers, but didn't move any farther away. Certainly not far enough that she could look into his eyes to see what he was thinking. He tipped his forehead down to hers, and for one long moment he waited, as if he were wondering if she had changed her mind.

Then he touched the pads of his fingertips to the satiny skin of her back one final time, and she could tell he was preparing to pull away. But when she realized his intention, she shoved her body more closely to his in a silent indication that he should continue.

So he did. Before she had a chance to think about what she had done, James dipped his head to the curve of her neck and shoulder, rubbing his lips gently over the soft skin there as he skimmed the zipper the rest of the way down. Little by little, the dress fell away from her body and his hands, pooling in a circle of black around her feet. Then he curled his fingers over the bare skin at the flare of her hips, and she heard him sigh with much contentment.

Kirby gripped his shirt in both fists and held on to him tight, burying her head against his chest, almost afraid of having him see her undressed. Again she could tell he was waiting for her to make the next move, as if he were torn between enjoying the erotic nature of the long, drawn-out moment and taking her as fiercely and immediately as she imagined his body was commanding him to do.

Surprisingly, she almost found herself wishing for a fast, demanding, primitive coupling, too. Her response to James came from within a well deep inside her that she had never tapped before. Although a part of her was terrified of what was about to happen, a part of her wondered what had taken her so long. That part of her—easily the largest part—was anxious to get on with it, eager to learn the secrets she had denied herself until now.

And she wanted James to be the one who shared the revelation with her.

"Kirby?" he asked softly as he settled his chin on the top of her head. "Is everything okay?"

She nodded silently, then boldly stepped out of her shoes, an action that left her wearing nothing but a pair of black silk panties and a black strapless bra. But still she clung to him, too worried to step away from him, because she feared he might find her lacking in some way. He'd been with a lot of women, she reminded herself, pushing away the melancholy that tried to accompany the thought. How could a woman making love for the first time possibly compare to some of the experiences James had enjoyed?

"I want to look at you," he told her. "I need to see you. Please."

"Couldn't we do this in the dark?" she mumbled against his chest.

He chuckled, and she was grateful to feel some of the tension leave her body at the sound. "Absolutely not. Haven't you accused me of being a Peeping Tom often enough?"

She nodded. "Among other things."

He seemed to sober some at the reminder. "Yeah, well, I plead guilty only to the Peeping Tom part," he told her. "What can I say? I'm a very visually oriented guy. Although," he added as he eased his hands between their bodies and covered her breasts with sure fingers, "there's a lot to be said for the sense of touch, too."

"Oh," she said softly as he closed his fingers more intently over her. "James, that's so...that feels so..."

She never finished what she was going to say, but she felt certain he pretty much understood the way she felt. The fact that her hands where shaking when she lifted her fingers to the top button of his shirt was no doubt another good indication.

"I suddenly find you to be overdressed," she told him, working free the first of his buttons.

"Need any help?" he asked, though he didn't remove his hands from her breasts.

She shook her head as she loosed the second button, but said nothing more, focusing all her concentration on his shirt. More than once, she nearly passed out from the pleasure of the sensation that hummed through her when James brushed his thumbs over the soft skin peeking out of her brassiere. And again when he weighed the heaviness of her breasts in his hands. And again when he rubbed his palm over each of the quickly ripening peaks.

His fingers found the front closure on her bra at the same time she began to tug his shirttail free of his trousers. Before he had a chance to loose the single hook that was all that held the frothy bit of black lace and satin in place, however, she took a step backward in a silent indication that he should remove his shirt.

And when he did, immediately, her gaze was drawn to the scattering of black hair sprayed across his chest, to every bump and ridge of abdominal muscle that he clearly took great pains to maintain, and then lower, to the zipper of his trousers.

Without comment, he reached for his belt and unbuckled it, then freed the length of leather and unbuttoned his pants. As Kirby watched, he drew down the second zipper of the evening. And all she could think then was that there was no way she would turn back now.

He hooked his thumbs in his waistband, paused long enough to toe off each of his shoes, then drew his trousers down over his long, muscular legs. He skimmed off his socks along with his pants, and then, like Kirby, stood wearing nothing but his underwear. In this case, a pair of black silk boxer shorts that did a very bad job of hiding how glad he was to see her. She marveled to think that she was the one responsible for the extent of his physical arousal. Had she really done that to him all by herself?

When she heard him chuckle, she glanced up at his face, and only then did she realize that she had been staring at him quite openly. But instead of blushing, as had been such a habit of hers in the past, she only smiled at him. She had expected to feel inhibited, bashful, uncertain, even frightened her first time. Yet with James she felt none of those things. During their time together, she had come to know him quite well, really better than any man of her acquaintance.

James had spoken freely, openly, honestly about himself. She wasn't sure she could say that about the other men she knew. As a result, she found that she felt no qualms about baring herself—both figuratively and literally—with him.

James smiled back when he understood her interest, a look of pure, unadulterated pride crossing his face. "You," he said softly, "are one sexy woman."

She shook her head in silent denial.

He nodded in response as he took a step forward and extended a hand toward her. "Trust me on this, Kirby. No woman has ever gotten a rise out of me—so to speak—faster than you have. All you have to do is look at me, or say my name a certain way, or just..." He chuckled softly. "Just walk into a room. Just the thought of you breathing somewhere on this planet turns me on."

She said nothing as she touched her fingertips to his, just let him pull her forward, against him. The sensation generated by the feel of his half-naked body pressed along the length of her own made her heart race with love, made her body tingle with wanting. The brush of his chest hair against her sensitive breasts, the brush of his fingers skimming over her bare back, the course of his lips along her neck and throat...

She gripped the hot satin of his upper arms to keep herself from falling, and realized vaguely that her fingers could only contain half the hard muscle flexing there. He was so big. So powerful. How would she ever be able to accommodate him?

Then she felt his mouth sweep lightly over the swell of her breast above her brassiere. He dipped his finger beneath the front closure and deftly unhooked it, then cast the froth of fabric away. And before she realized his intention, his warm, wet mouth closed over one nipple, and Kirby's knees buckled beneath her.

James caught her capably, winding one strong arm around her waist as he cradled her breast with the other hand. Without missing a beat, he pushed the soft mound up to his mouth, then circled the dusky peak with his tongue before drawing her more fully inside.

Kirby cried out at the explosion of dizzying heat that crashed through her, the powerful suction of his mouth creating a rhythm that mimicked the beating of her heart. He licked her with the flat of his tongue, tickled her with the tip, and all she could do was wind her fingers through the silky length of his hair and hold on tight.

But instead of satisfying his thirst, James's taste of her only seemed to intensify his need. He moved to her other breast, treating it to the same ministrations, his mouth hungrier now, more demanding, more needy. And she responded to that hunger and demand with an appetite equally voracious.

She uttered his name on a gasp, and in reply, he swept her up into his arms and kissed her deeply again. She linked her hands behind his neck and kissed him back, her lips fighting with his for dominion, their tongues battling for possession. She didn't realize where he was headed until she felt the cool cotton of the sheets against the heated flesh on her back, but even then, the assault continued.

James came down on top of her, bracing the bulk of his weight on the elbows he settled on each side of her head. The weight of him atop her excited Kirby more than anything else that had come before, and she hooked her legs over his to lock him to herself. Again she was nearly overcome by the feel of him pressing against her from head to toe, and she fancied they were almost fused into one being.

Then James tore his mouth away from hers and began a slow exploration downward, tasting her neck, her shoulder, her breasts, her ribs, then lower still, dipping a quick kiss into her navel.

"James," she whispered when she realized he had left her, "what are you doing? Where are you going?"

She glanced down to find that he had nestled his entire body between her legs, and had curled the fingers of both hands into the waistband of her panties. She also noticed that there was a wicked, wicked gleam in his eyes.

"You want me to make love to you, don't you?" he asked.

She nodded but said nothing, not certain she trusted her voice.

"Did I neglect to mention that I'm a very...thorough...lover?" he asked, the wicked, wicked gleam in his eyes moving lower to become a wicked, wicked smile.

She nodded again.

"Well, then," he said softly, giving her panties a tug. "Consider yourself warned."

"James, what are you going to...?"

She halted when he pulled her panties off her hips, over her legs, and discarded them on the floor. Then slowly, very slowly he began to lower his head to the damp, heated heart of her. Her eyes widened in both shock and trepidation. He wasn't, she thought. He wouldn't, she told herself. He couldn't.

He did.

Before she could voice her objection, his mouth covered the sensitive folds of flesh between her legs, and he moved his tongue against her more softly than a butterfly's wings, stabbing at that most sensitive part of her, tasting her more intimately than she ever would have imagined. And by then she could say nothing at all. Nothing except...

"Oh, *James*..."

He chuckled low, then pressed a palm against each thigh and opened her wider for his invasion. Over and over again his head descended, his mouth maneuvered and his tongue danced against her. Kirby threw her head back against the pillow, curled her fingers tightly in the sheets and let herself be carried away by the ecstasy that swept her away. Over and over and over again.

And just when she thought she could tolerate no more, she felt James beside her again, pulling her toward himself, his mouth at her throat, his hand cupping her breast, his muscular thigh resting between her own. As she had earlier, she instinctively moved against him, thrusting her hips forward over the hot, hard flesh of his leg. Only, this time, there was no barrier of clothing to inhibit her pleasure. And this time the friction of her skin against his was almost more than she could bear.

Almost.

Then James rolled her onto her back and lay atop her again, once more bracing himself on his elbows. This time, however, instead of kissing her, he cupped her face in his hands and gazed down into her eyes. She felt the hard fullness of him pressing against her belly, and she wondered again how she would ever be able to take all of him inside herself. Then, as a surprising serenity washed over her, she realized she was about to find out.

To James, there had never been a more beautiful, more sensuous, more responsive woman than the one he held in his arms right now. Kirby's reaction to his lovemaking tonight had been completely unpracticed, totally artless, entirely without pretense. No man had ever touched her or tasted her the way he had touched and tasted her tonight. The knowledge of that brought with it a staggering sense of something he'd never felt before. Whatever she had said and done in response to him had been natural, basic, genuine. As had been, he was amazed to realize, his reaction to her.

"Kirby," he said softly, his heart racing at the sparkle of emotion in her eyes. "Are you absolutely sure this is what you want?"

Part of him honestly hoped she would say no, it wasn't what she wanted and she had to leave right now. But when she nodded her head in silent assent, satisfaction bloomed to life inside him. He flattened his palm against her belly and scooted his hand lower, burying his fingers in the damp warmth he had so recently tasted. She was wet, hot, eager for him. When he probed her with a gentle finger, gradually deepening the penetration, she closed her eyes and sighed with delight. And when a second finger joined the first, she thrust her hips up to greet him.

She was small and tight, but she was slick and opening for his possession. Then he felt her fingers brushing against him, skimming lightly over his hard shaft, exploring, investigating. This time he was the one to squeeze his eyes shut and sigh with delight, silently encouraging her to roam at her leisure. The tentative touch of her hand running along his heavy length was nearly his undoing, though. And fearful that he would respond too quickly, he circled her wrist with gentle fingers and pulled her hand away. She seemed to understand, because she smiled at him and withdrew her fingers from him.

"Do you want me to go slow?" he asked when he could find his voice. "Or would you rather I go fast?"

She studied his face for a long time before responding, and his heart hammered hard in his chest at the tumble of emotions that shot through him as he watched her. "Fast, I think," she finally said. "I really want to feel you inside me. Now."

He swallowed hard, both grateful for her decision—he really wanted to be inside her, too—and dismayed by it. He didn't want to hurt her. But he knew there was little chance of avoiding that. Still, if Kirby wanted it to go quickly, then he would abide by her request. Had she asked him for the moon right then, he would have reached into the sky to seize it for her.

She watched without inhibition as he pulled away from her long enough to sheathe himself in a condom, then extended her arms toward him in invitation. James came to her willingly, covered her body with his and, fastening his gaze to hers, he entered her.

Quickly, deeply, resolutely. She closed her eyes and cried out as he breached the final barrier of her innocence, and a single, fat tear streamed from each of her eyes. The sight of her tears stirred something inside him from a profound sleep, and he swiftly, gently thumbed them away. For one long moment, Kirby lay silent and still beneath him with her eyes closed, her chest heaving raggedly for air, her fingers clenched into fists against his back, her legs wrapped tightly around his.

And then she moved against him. She urged her hips forward ever so slightly, and James finally released the breath he had been holding. Slowly, noting the way she bit her lip in what he hoped was ecstasy instead of agony, he withdrew some from her. Then he pushed himself forward, slowly, this time, until he was deep inside her again. She was so tight, so snug around him, something that only magnified his own enjoyment. He forced himself to set a steady, easy pace, speeding up only when she began to relax.

But almost as soon as she relaxed, her body tensed again, this time in response to the pleasure instead of the pain. Little by little, they climbed higher toward completion. Faster and faster he thrust himself inside her. Harder and harder she drove herself up to meet him. Until finally, an explosion in the white-hot extreme burned them both down to their cores.

As one, they cried out at the peak of their euphoria, reveled in the culmination of their union, marveled at the newness of the feelings that overcame them. Then James collapsed against Kirby, exhausted by the totality of the experience. Everything. Suddenly she was *everything* to him. Nothing mattered in that moment but Kirby. He had never experienced such a sensation before. And the realization of that was simply too overwhelming for him to think about right now.

So he rolled from atop her, settled to her side and pulled her back against him, shushing her when she tried to speak, holding her still when she tried to turn to face him.

"Sleep," he whispered, barely able to put voice to that one

word. "Tomorrow," he managed to add, hoping she would understand.

She must have, because she nestled against him with much affection, draping an arm back over his waist. James looped his own over her hip, cupping her thigh possessively. Then, emptying his mind of everything but the sound of her, the scent of her, the feel of her, he closed his eyes and slept.

Kirby awoke to a pleasant sort of achiness and a very enjoyable lethargy. Parts of her that had lain dormant and unnoticed in the past were stirring to life with her waking, tingling, warming, wanting satisfaction, warring with other parts of her that urged her to just lie still and go back to sleep. But ultimately she realized that sleep was the last thing she wanted right now. No, what she wanted right now, more than anything else, was for James to wake up, smile brightly, make love to her again, and then...

And then ask her to marry him.

Unfortunately, she was just conscious enough to remember his vow of the night before, the one in which he'd made it more than clear that such a thing just wasn't going to happen.

She opened her eyes and rolled over, only to find him lying beside her, still sound asleep, oblivious to all the turmoil that was knotting inside her. Last night she had made love for the first time, something that, in a matter of moments, had changed her completely and irrevocably. She wasn't the Kirby Connaught she had been twenty-four hours ago, and she would never be that woman again. And not just because of the physical ramifications of her new status, either. But because of the emotional ones.

She did love James. More now that they'd made love than she had before—something she wouldn't have thought was possible. And she would always love him, she knew. Forever after. Wish come true. Score one for the comet. And thanks so much for playing.

Nice going, Bob, she thought sadly.

James, too, began to stir then, inhaling deeply as he woke, and she experienced a brief moment of panic. She drew the sheet up over her breasts and held it snugly to herself, a whirlwind of questions carousing in her brain. What happened to two people after they made love? What was she supposed to do now? What was she supposed to say? How was she supposed to act? Would James behave differently toward her? Would he be expecting something in particular?

But when he opened his eyes and smiled warmly at her, all Kirby's worries dissolved, and she smiled back. He lifted a hand to her face and touched a fingertip to her cheek, then traced it down to her mouth, over her lower lip. Impulsively she kissed his thumb as it passed, and he laughed lightly. Then he heaved himself up on one elbow, pushed his long hair away from his face, and smiled at her some more.

"Good morning," he said softly.

Warmth wound through her entire body at the sound of his sleep-roughened voice. "Good morning yourself."

As if he were unable to keep from touching her, he skimmed his fingers lightly down her throat, along her collarbone, then over her bare arm and back up again. His touch brought with it a soft heat that uncoiled in her belly, spreading slowly to every extreme. Kirby lifted her own hand and threaded her fingers lightly through his hair, marveling at the softness of the silk tresses as they sifted through her fingers.

Oh, how she would miss him when he was gone.

When his eyes met hers, concern darkened their gray depths. "Are you okay?" he asked quietly. "Did I...did I hurt you last night?"

She grazed her hand down to cup his jaw gingerly in her palm. She didn't want to lie to him, but she didn't want to give him the wrong impression, either. "Only at first," she finally told him. "And only for a minute," she hastened to add when she saw his crestfallen expression. "James, I..." She quickly bit her lip to keep herself from blurting out all the things she wanted to tell him. Things he undoubtedly didn't want to hear.

"What?" he asked, still grazing his fingertips along the length of her bare arm.

She shook her head. "Nothing. Never mind. Last night was..." She sighed, a wistful sound, and dropped her hand to tangle her fingers in the soft hair of his chest. "It was amazing," she finished quietly. "No one could have made it more special than you did."

He studied her intently, his fingers pausing in their motion, his thoughts obviously tied up with things at which she could only guess. "Are you sure?" he asked.

"Yes," she told him honestly. "I'll never forget it." She hesitated only briefly before adding, "And I'll never forget you, either."

Something clouded his features then, too quickly for her to discern exactly what. She waited for him to say something, but he remained silent. It wasn't a good sign, she thought. But then, what had she expected?

"I, um..." she began, feeling awkward in her nudity for the first time since last night. She pulled the sheet more snugly around her torso. "I should probably go."

His eyebrows drifted downward at that. "Go? Why? I didn't think we had any more functions until tomorrow."

"Not for the festival," she clarified. "But I have to, um... I have to go to a wedding today."

Now his eyebrows arched upward in surprise. The effect would have been comical, Kirby thought, if it weren't for the cold block of ice that had settled in her stomach.

"Who's getting married?" he asked.

"My friend Angie."

"The one who breaks into mobsters' houses?"

Kirby nodded, smiling in spite of the sudden tension that was tightening the air between them. "That's the one. Only, today she's marrying the mobster."

James's expression would have been the same if she had poked him in the eye. "Why am I just now finding out about this?" he asked.

She shrugged. "Because you never asked?"

He hardened his gaze, but didn't comment. So she relented some. "It's a very, very, *very* long story. But what it boils down to is that Bob has granted Angie's wish. In spades. She wanted something exciting, and *boy*, did she get that."

Kirby dropped her gaze down to the bed, her heart hammering harder when she noted the tiny red stain she saw there. She tugged on the sheet until the stain was covered, hoping her gesture went unnoticed. Then she glanced back up to see that James had been watching her every move. So she looked away again.

"And I think he's giving her my wish, too," she added morosely, having figured out pretty well what was going on with Angie and her mobster, even if Angie was still totally clueless herself.

"A wedding, huh?" James asked. When Kirby glanced over at him again, his expression was shuttered, and his voice belied nothing of what he might be thinking or feeling. "So it'll be the old ball and chain, then, eh?"

"It will be a joyful union." She begged to differ.

"It'll be a leash around the neck, you mean."

"No, I mean it will be two people making official their love forever after," she countered, a wide, aching hole opening up in the pit of her stomach at his colorful assertions to the contrary.

But instead of arguing further, James only said, "Angie's in love with a mobster, is she?"

Kirby nodded, but didn't argue the point. What was the point of arguing about the existence of love to someone who didn't believe in it? Then, on a whim, she asked him, "Would you like to go with me? The invitation said I could bring a date. I would have asked you before, but I didn't think you'd want to attend something like a wedding. They're pretty personal and all that."

She didn't dare look up at him, for fear of what she would see in his eyes. So instead, she only tangled her fingers in the sheet and waited for his answer. And waited. And waited. And waited.

"I don't think so," he finally said. But he offered no other explanation.

Any hope she had embraced that he might change his mind about staying with her in Endicott died with his casual declining of her invitation. Hey, he'd spelled it out for her perfectly last night, she reminded herself. He'd told her flat out that he wasn't built to love her for anything other than the short run. He'd spent the last two weeks making clear just what kind of man he was. She'd known from the start that he was neither the love-forever-after kind of guy, nor the answer to a fifteen-year-old wish.

He was James Nash. World traveler. Cultural icon. Lover of women. Breaker of hearts. And it would take more than a comet with a sick sense of humor to change that.

"Okay," she said, amazed that she could keep her voice steady when she was falling apart inside.

She moved to the edge of the mattress, pulling the sheet with her, wrapping herself in it like a mummy. Her clothes were still scattered on the floor, and she realized she was going to look plenty foolish leaving the hotel at ten in the morning dressed in her rumpled cocktail dress of the night before.

Oh, well, she tried to reassure herself as she collected her things. It would give the gossips more to talk about. There should be no question around town now that she was damaged goods. Yes, sir, the boys ought to start lining up at her front door this very evening, wanting their chance to have a go at her. Wasn't that what she had wanted all along?

She had gathered the last of her things and was almost to the bathroom when James called out her name. She turned to find him lying exactly as he had been when she'd risen from bed, his back to her now, his face to the wall.

"I, uh," he began quietly without even bothering to turn around, "I think I'm going to cut my trip short. I'll be leaving Endicott this afternoon."

Something dry and bitter welled up inside her, and she honestly wasn't sure she'd be able to speak. But she cleared her throat and gave it a shot anyway. "This afternoon?" she echoed. "But tonight's the night Bob will be making his closest pass to Earth. I would have thought you'd want to be here for that."

He still hadn't turned around to look at her, still lay gazing at the wall instead. "Yeah, but...I think I've seen all I want to see."

He might as well have slapped her, so cold and profound was the betrayal that knifed through her. Kirby closed her eyes at the intensity of the pain. Try as she might, she couldn't think of a single thing to say. So she ducked into the bathroom, splashed some cold water on her face, dressed as quickly as she could and exited again.

She had intended to leave without looking back, without a further word, without any indication of just how deeply he had wounded her. But as she gripped the doorknob, she realized she simply could not leave things the way they were. James Nash had been her first lover, her first love. For the rest of her life, he would remain her first—he might perhaps even be her only. And she refused to have her first time sullied by a hurtful farewell.

So she spun around to find that he had risen from bed and dressed in a burgundy silk robe, and was standing near the window beside a telescope much larger than what the average amateur stargazer claimed. And she realized two things in succession. Number one, she knew now how he had been able to see her naked that first day. And number two, she knew that no matter what he had just said to her, she would always love him.

"I'll miss you, James," she told him quietly.

As if he were no longer able to keep himself aloof, he turned at her softly uttered declaration. From the distance that separated them, it was impossible for her to tell what he was thinking. But still he said nothing, and her heart sank even more.

"And I'll always remember you fondly," she added.

He dropped his gaze to the ground, guiltily, she thought for some reason. But he continued to remain silent.

She'd come this far, she told herself. He'd be leaving in a few hours, and she'd never see him again. "I'm glad you were my first," she told him, twisting the knob to pull the door open. She took one step forward, then another, and another, until she was almost clear of the hotel suite.

Then, unable to help herself, before she slammed the door closed behind her, she said over her shoulder, "I'm glad, because not everyone can say they were in love their first time. But I can."

And then she was gone. Just like James. Forever after.

Ten

Angie's wedding went off without a hitch, save the stunned, incredulous look on the bride's face immediately following the minister's announcement that she and the handsome man beside her were husband and wife. Regardless of her friend's reaction, Kirby was still convinced that things between Angie and Ethan Zorn were going to work out nicely. The way those two looked at each other told the whole story. They were in love—that's all there was to it. A forever-after kind of love if ever there was one, whether they were willing to admit it or not.

If only they could all convince Ethan to enter another line of work....

Now, as Kirby stood at the front of the group crowding the reception hall of the Elks Lodge, she smiled faintly at the sight of the bride and groom feeding each other wedding cake. And she found herself wishing that James had looked at her just once the way Ethan was looking at Angie. Had James offered her even one small indication that he felt as strongly, as lovingly about her as Ethan clearly felt about his new bride, then Kirby would have stayed in James's hotel room until the end of time.

Of course, she thought further, glancing down at her watch, if she'd done that, then she would have been staying there alone by now. It was nearly four-thirty. James was no doubt sitting in the first-class section of a jumbo jet, on his way to some international playground, with a woman on his arm who would be far more entertaining than some little virgin from Indiana.

Then again, she reminded herself, she wasn't a virgin anymore, was she?

She glanced down at her dress, a big puffy-sleeved, drop-waist number nearly overcome with billowing pink cabbage roses and pearl buttons. Even back in her old, favored attire, she didn't feel at all the way she used to feel about herself. She felt more womanly, more worldly, more experienced, more human. Not because she had lost her virginity. But because she had known the full depth of true love, and had lost it.

"Kirby?"

She turned to find Teddy Gundersen smiling at her, looking handsome and all-American dressed in his JCPenney suit and his Adidas sneakers, his fingers wrapped around a can of Budweiser. He was the kind of man who was much more appropriate for her way of life. He had grown up in Endicott, had played quarterback for Endicott Central High School, had graduated from the community college with a degree in marketing and was well situated at the Peter Piper Pickle Plant.

He'd make a good husband and father, she told herself. The two of them could have a whole passel of blond, blue-eyed kids he could coach at soccer. So why, suddenly, did she have absolutely no desire to get to know him better?

"You're not here with James Nash?" he asked.

She shook her head. "No. He, um, he had to leave."

The other man looked surprised. "Before the end of the festival? But he's the grand marshal, and there's still a week to go. Besides, I thought you and he…?" His voice trailed up at the end of his observation, but he said nothing further.

Kirby scrunched up her shoulders and pretended not to notice that part of his statement. "Apparently James was needed somewhere else a lot more than we needed him here in Endicott. We can do without a grand marshal for the remainder of the festival."

Although, of course, there was going to be a real feeling of incompletion now. But then, overall, that was rather appropriate, wasn't it?

Teddy nodded, his expression warming as he asked, "So...you wanna dance?"

There was nothing even remotely suggestive or improper in his voice or the question, nor in his face as he posed it. She realized then that although James had definitely acted as a catalyst in making the single men of Endicott view her in a new light, he hadn't ruined her reputation at all. No one present at Angie's wedding had treated Kirby any differently than they had before, even though many had commented on her liaison with James. In their eyes, she was still the town good girl, she realized. She just wasn't the local virgin anymore.

She shook her head lightly and smiled at Teddy. "No, thanks," she told him. "I need to find Rosemary before Angie and Ethan leave."

He nodded and smiled back. "Would it be okay if I called you sometime?"

She wanted to decline, having no desire to meet socially with anyone right now. She knew it was unlikely that she'd be in the mood to date for the next fifty or sixty years. So she only replied vaguely, "If you want."

He nodded and started to turn away, then pointed to something behind Kirby. Her heart began to pound fiercely, and she chastised herself for hoping that the person he had spied was James, who had found his way to the wedding in an effort to locate her.

But what Teddy said was, "Here comes Rosemary with Angie now."

Her heart sank as she turned, and she berated herself for ever getting her hopes up. James was gone, she reminded herself. And there was nothing in the world that would bring him back to Endicott.

"We're leaving," Angie said without ceremony.

Kirby's eyebrows shot up in surprise. "Leaving? But what about Ethan? You're his wife now."

Angie narrowed her eyes in confusion. "No, I meant 'we' as

in Ethan and I are leaving, not Rosemary and I. He and I are headed over to the hotel.''

"Oh.''

"But I'm headed out, too,'' Rosemary added. "Willis and I are going home now that the party's winding down.''

Kirby nodded. Angie was headed to the honeymoon suite at the Admiralty Inn, and Rosemary was headed back to her house, where she and Willis were living together, however reluctantly. And where was Kirby headed? Home alone to toast the fact that Bob had granted all three of their wishes, with a bottle of expensive champagne she'd stolen from the man she loved.

Funny that all she had left of James was a pilfered symbol of celebration that would quickly go flat once she uncorked it. Somehow it just seemed appropriate.

"Have fun, you guys,'' she muttered.

Both her friends hesitated, each of them eyeing her with much suspicion.

"Um, Kirb,'' Angie said, "are you okay? You seem different today somehow. And I'm not referring to the fact that you've obviously abandoned all those ridiculous outfits you've been wearing. I mean you seem...'' She paused, as if searching for the right word. "I don't know. Different. From before. From before James Nash came to town.''

Rosemary, too, seemed to be taking an unusually long perusal of Kirby, and nodded her agreement. "Yeah, like you're, um... Like you're not quite, uh...'' She gaped suddenly, the color draining from her face. "You did it, didn't you?''

Kirby felt her old color rise to the surface quickly. "Did what?'' she asked.

Angie, too, was staring at her openmouthed. "You didn't,'' she said.

"Didn't what?'' Kirby asked, still hedging.

"Oh, my God...'' the other two women said as one, identical grins of delight spreading across their faces.

"You did *it*,'' Angie charged. "It. *It.*''

"You finally lost it, didn't you?'' Rosemary asked.

"With James Nash?'' Angie clarified.

Kirby smiled sadly, oddly pleased that she would seem different now. "Yeah, I, um...I lost it with James Nash," she said softly. Lost her virginity, lost her heart.

Angie nodded, looking for the first time that day the way a bride should look at the prospect of marital bliss. Then she gripped the bouquet of white roses in one hand, untied the ivory ribbon binding the blossoms together with the other, and deftly divided them into three smaller bunches.

"Aren't you supposed to throw that?" Kirby asked her.

"Not a chance," she replied. "It's my wedding. I'll give my bouquet to whoever I damn well please. Here. One for you," she said as she handed a fragrant bunch to Rosemary. "And one for you," she added, offering another to Kirby. "And one for me." She wound the ribbon back around the now shrunken bridal bouquet. "I gotta go," she said, crooking her finger in farewell. "My, uh..." She cleared her throat indelicately. "My husband is waiting for me."

And with that, Angie left her friends staring first down at the broken bridal bouquet in their hands, and then after their departing friend.

"I, uh...I have to go, too," Rosemary said, gesturing with the roses toward a tall, handsome man dressed in tweed who was watching her from the other side of the room. "Willis is waiting for me."

Kirby nodded as she carefully fingered the delicate white blossoms in her own hand. "Go ahead," she said, glancing down at the sweet-smelling, if incomplete, bouquet.

The encouragement was unnecessary, because Rosemary had already taken a few steps away. She hesitated however, and asked, "Kirby? Are you going to be okay?"

Kirby nodded but said nothing, only continued to gaze down at the perfect white roses she held in her hand.

"Oh, yeah," Rosemary added then, something in her voice having lightened. "I see that you *are* going to be okay. See ya later. Have fun."

Have fun? That was a good one. "See ya," she said softly.

When Kirby glanced up to offer a halfhearted wave to her other departing friend, she saw Rosemary's back disappearing through the door on the other side of the room, beside the broad, tweed-covered shoulders of Willis Random. And then Kirby's heart nearly stopped. Because another man still lingered in the doorway.

James Nash.

Dressed in an elegant black tuxedo, his ivory collarless shirt studded with ebony buttons, his jet hair bound at his nape, a white rose fastened in his lapel, he simply leaned against the doorjamb, hands in his pockets, gazing at her. As was, she realized with some apprehension, everyone else in the room.

When he saw that he had her attention, he smiled, a smile so soft, she could swear he meant for her to be the only one who saw it. Then he pushed himself away from the door and sauntered forward, his steps never faltering, never slowing, until he stood right in front of her.

"Hi," he said simply, as if they were meeting again for the first time.

"Hi," she responded automatically. At last her heart started beating again, but with a rapid, dizzying pace that made her feel woozy. The silence surrounding them was an awesome thing, as if everyone in Endicott stood waiting to see what would happen with the virgin and the vagabond.

James glanced around at their surroundings, nodding his head vaguely at their audience. Then he turned his attention back to Kirby and asked, "Am I too late for the wedding?"

She nodded, her gaze never leaving his. She was afraid that if she looked away, even for a moment, he would disappear, retreating into her fantasies. "Angie and Ethan just left," she said.

He smiled again, this time that toe-curling smile that had tied her in knots from day one. "No, not that wedding. The other wedding."

Kirby narrowed her eyes, confused. "What other wedding?"

"There's another one scheduled for five o'clock at city hall," he told her.

"But it's Saturday," she pointed out. "City hall is closed."

He lifted one shoulder in an idle shrug. "Not if you're an international celebrity who counts the mayor among his fans, it's not."

Kirby's heart skidded to a halt, then began to thunder double-time. She just couldn't quite believe he was telling her what he seemed to be telling her. "So...whose wedding would that be?" she finally managed to say.

He smiled again, then extracted his hands from his pockets and extended one toward her, revealing a small, black velvet box settled in his palm. "Our wedding."

Her breath caught in her throat when he opened the box, and there, nestled in a crush of more black velvet, was a perfect, heart-shaped diamond. Not too big, not too little, just perfect for a small-town woman with high standards and a good reputation.

When she looked up at James, he'd gone all blurry, and for a moment, she thought her fears had come true, that he was dissolving back into her dreams. Then she felt a damp warmth on her cheeks. She blinked and her vision cleared, but only until her eyes filled with tears again.

"Oh, James..."

She hurtled herself against him, wrapping her arms around his neck with all her might, pressing her mouth to his with a ferocity and longing known only to people who were irrevocably in love—a forever-after kind of love that spans all time. What was even better, though, was that James kissed her back with that exact same ferocity and longing.

He held her close, folded his arms over her back, lifted her off the ground and into his embrace and slanted his mouth more fully over hers. For long moments, they stood so entwined, as if they would never get enough of each other, oblivious to the cheers and applause of the delighted onlookers who urged them on.

When it finally dawned on Kirby that they had such an avid audience, she blushed and pulled away—for breath, for reassurance...for clarification.

"Why?" she said as she looped her arms fiercely around his neck, the single word all she was able to manage.

He chuckled in response...nervously and with much uncertainty, she noted. Then he swallowed hard. "What do you mean, 'why?' Don't you want to marry me?"

"Are you nuts? Of course I do."

His expression cleared dramatically with her agreement, and

only then did she realize he had been worried she would say no. Laughter bubbled up inside her.

"I just meant..." She tried again. "This morning...in your room, I thought... I thought you... Um—"

"Yeah, well, I *wasn't* thinking," he interrupted, sparing her from having to relive an experience she had no desire to revisit ever again. "I was too busy panicking to be thinking."

She shook her head slowly. "I don't understand."

James inhaled deeply and pulled Kirby more fully into his arms, reveling in the warmth and the scent of lavender that surrounded him with her nearness. He couldn't believe how close he had come to losing her, to missing out on the one thing he had always wanted in life, just because he had been too blind to see what should have been as plain as a fireball whizzing through the night sky. But it hadn't been until he'd heard Kirby say that she loved him that he finally understood what had happened.

"The last time Bob came around," he began again, tightening his arms around her waist, "I was fifteen years old, too."

Kirby smiled, obviously delighted by the realization. "You were born in the year of the comet?"

He nodded, smiling back. "Not in Endicott, like you, but yes. I was born in the year of Bob. Maybe that's why I've always been so fascinated by comets. Whatever the reason, by the time I was fifteen, I knew all about Bob. I knew about the legends surrounding him, and I knew about the myth of the wishes. And the last time Bob came around, I looked up into the sky and I made a wish, too."

Her smile grew dreamy, and the fingers twined at his nape loosened, to delve affectionately into the ponytail fixed above them. "You did?"

He nodded again. "I wasn't in Endicott at the time. I was in Spain with my parents, on a train somewhere between Seville and Córdoba." He grimaced at the memory. "It was the middle of the night, and my parents were arguing, quite frankly and without concern for my presence, about my mother's latest boyfriend and my father's latest astrologer. And while they hurled insults and threats at each other, I began to feel very, very alone."

"Oh, James."

"And I looked out the window of the sleeper car—" he rushed on before she could say anything more "—up at a bright spot in the sky that I knew was Bob, and I made a wish. The kind of wish only a lonely, fifteen-year-old boy being dragged through a foreign country he had no desire to visit in the first place can make."

She hesitated for a moment before asking, "What did you wish for?"

He gazed down into her face, then lifted a hand from her back and knifed his fingers gently through her hair. "I wished that I could live a normal, happy life with people who loved me," he said softly. "I wished I could be a normal person with normal experiences and a normal family, instead of the son of a couple of rich, vagabond hedonists who cared more about satisfying their own eccentric appetites than they did about their only child.

"I wished I was happy, Kirby," he added more softly. "I wished someone would love me for who I am. That was what I wanted Bob to bring me."

"Oh, James..."

"But naturally, since I wasn't born in Endicott, and since I wasn't standing in Endicott when I made my wish, I knew it would never come true." He brushed his open hand over her hair again, cradling the back of her head in his palm, urging her forward to press his forehead against hers.

"And my wish didn't come true," he added. "Not until I actually came to Endicott. But the day I set foot here, Bob granted my wish. He gave me you, Kirby. You're my wish come true."

"Oh, James..."

He laughed softly, then dipped his head to kiss her mouth, briefly, lovingly. "Is that all you're going to say for the rest of your life? 'Oh, James'?"

She made a soft, little hiccuping sound, swiped quickly at her eyes and said, "Oh, James..." Then she laughed, too, and crowded herself against him again.

"This morning, when I heard you say you love me, it suddenly all became clear. It was all so simple, right there in front of me. I'd just been too blind to see it."

She nestled her head against his chest and spread her hand open over his heart. "Well, I'm sorry," she said softly, "but it's not that clear and simple to me, so you'll have to spell it out for me."

He chuckled as he enfolded her in his arms. "I'm saying that Endicott, Indiana, is about as normal a place as you can find. People are happy here. So happy that they don't feel compelled to tear a piece off of someone—literally—just because that person is a cultural icon. I could live a normal, happy life here, Kirby."

"Because of the people in Endicott?" she asked.

He shook his head. "Because of *one* person in Endicott. One person who loves me for who I am. You."

"And here I've been accusing you all along of being nothing but a promiscuous playboy Peeping Tom," she said.

He chuckled again. "That's because I tried to make you think that's what I was. But you saw right through me."

She chuckled, too. "Gee, I guess I did. And I fell in love with the wonderful man beneath."

"I love you, too, Kirby," he vowed, settling his chin at the crown of her head. "I couldn't tell you before, because I didn't realize it. I didn't recognize the feeling. I'd never loved anyone before. But after you left this morning, when I was standing there all alone in my hotel room... The emptiness that overcame me, the thought of not having you around, of never seeing you again... It was horrible. And terrifying. And I never want to feel that way again. Marry me. Please."

For one long moment, she said nothing. She only glanced up to meet his gaze with tear-filled eyes and tangle her hands in his hair. Then she smiled, kissed him again and said, "Well, okay. If that's what it takes to make you happy."

James smiled, too, then moved away to pluck the ring from its velvet nest and slide it over the fourth finger of her left hand. He watched as she considered it in the light, turning her hand first left, then right, loving the way her features softened as she did so.

"It's beautiful," she told him.

"No, you're beautiful," he replied.

She smiled shyly up at him, then returned her attention to the ring. "It sparkles like crazy."

"It's full of fire."

"Like Bob," she said with a laugh.

"Like my love for you," he countered.

She cupped her hands behind his neck again and pushed herself up on tiptoe to kiss him. "I love you, James," she told him softly.

"And I love you, Kirby. Now then, let's go get married and lead a normal, happy, loving life."

They couldn't get the honeymoon suite at the Admiralty Inn that night, because it was already occupied. So they went to Kirby's house instead.

Frankly, James didn't care where they went, as long as he was with Kirby. He knew he'd never have to circle the globe again, following a quest for adventure and the extraordinary in exotic locales. Because he'd finally defined that elusive something he'd been searching for all his adult life. Better yet, he'd found it. Fulfillment. Happiness. Contentment. Love. And he'd discovered it all in Endicott, Indiana.

He'd discovered it all with Kirby.

Now the only thing he cared about as he carried his wife over the threshold of a pink stucco house on Oak Street was getting naked with her as soon as he possibly could. Fortunately for him, Kirby seemed to have the same idea, because the minute he kicked the door shut behind them, she began working furiously at the buttons on his shirt. So what could James do but return the favor?

"You know," he said, torn between setting her down to undress her and holding her in his arms this way forever, "it occurs to me that you're my wife, and I don't even know where your bedroom is."

Kirby glanced up from where her fingers were wrestling with a particularly stubborn stud. "Down the hall, last door on the right," she said before returning to her efforts.

He curved his hand more possessively over her fanny, tugged her close and made his way in that direction. The color scheme in Kirby's bedroom was as soft and soothing as elsewhere in the house—a mossy green on the walls, accented by a gauzy ivory bedspread, a flowered hooked rug and an overstuffed club chair that he made a mental note of making love in later. The setting sun, nearly finished for the day, bathed the room in pale golden light, giving it the impression of warmth that having Kirby close only intensified.

James set his wife down at the center of it all and, with great glee, reached for the pink satin bow beneath her big white collar.

"It was really nice of Mayor March to open city hall on a Saturday and rush through all that annoying premarital paperwork just for us," he said as he moved to the buttons beneath. "I didn't want to wait one more day to get married."

Kirby laughed as she freed two of his buttons at once. "Yeah, and was it nice of her to alert the media beforehand to have our nuptials blasted via satellite all over the globe? I mean, I know Mrs. March is eager to advertise Endicott and all that, but still..."

She tugged his shirttail from his trousers and loosed the last button. "Although, now that I think about it, now that everyone on the planet has witnessed your wedding, they'll all know you're taken by me forever after, and you won't be the Most Desirable Man in America anymore."

"Oh, I'll be a desirable man in America," he countered, his nimble fingers skimming lower on her button placket. "Especially in Indiana."

"Yes, well, that goes without saying. But it's only because I love you, James. Don't forget that."

"Forever after," he agreed with an avid nod. "Just like my love for you."

At last, at last, he had freed enough of her little pearl buttons to shove the dress down over her hips, leaving it in a pool of pink cabbage roses around her ankles. Then, when he straightened, his breath caught in his throat at the sight of what she had on beneath it.

Under her very prim, very old-fashioned, very baggy dress, Kirby wore a shell pink teddy, laced loosely up over breasts that were half spilling from a matching demicup bra. Attached to the mist of lace with frothy garters were white silk stockings.

"My God," he said. "Is that what you've been wearing under those dresses all this time?"

She lifted a shoulder in matter-of-fact acknowledgment, a gesture that made her breasts dance in their skimpy confinement. Oh, boy.

"Well, yeah," she said softly.

"Are you serious?" he asked, nearly strangling on the question, still staring at the utterly revealing, impossibly feminine, totally erotic lingerie.

She nodded, biting her lip. "You don't like it?"

He gaped at her. "Like it? Kirby..."

Instead of trying to tell her what her choice of underthings did to him, James decided to show her. He reached for her, pulled her toward himself and kissed her soundly. And while he did, she shoved his shirt and jacket as one from his shoulders, then went to work on his belt. In no time at all, he stood before her clad as scantily as she in his black silk boxers, flesh heating, hearts pounding, libidos raging.

Had someone told him a month ago that he would feel such indecent, incandescent things for an innocent from Indiana, James would have laughed in that person's face. But at the moment, all he wanted was to relive that incredible heat he had shared with Kirby the night before. Tonight, however, he wanted her to feel nothing but joy. No pain, no inhibition, no doubt. Only love, only ecstasy, only the two of them coming together as one.

"This time, you call the shots," he told her when he finally managed to tear his mouth free of hers. "You're not inexperienced anymore. This time, it's all up to you."

Her response to his request was a suggestive little smile. Then she took a few oh-so-casual steps away from him, lifted her hand to the ribbon that closed her skimpy teddy and said, "I think, first, I'd like to take these things off."

James nodded agreeably. "Okay. That's fine with me."

Very, very gently, she tugged on the pink ribbon until the bow unlooped. Then very, very slowly, she unlaced herself, spreading wide the wispy fabric once the ribbon was free. She reached for one strap and flipped it over her shoulder, then performed the same gesture on the other side. Down over her arms and elbows fell the cotton candy confection of lace and silk, and with a little shimmy that sent her entire body into motion, Kirby disengaged it from her arms completely. She left it bunched around her waist as she reached behind herself to unfasten her bra. Then, when she completed the action, she crossed her arms over herself in what was clearly feigned modesty.

James watched her every move as if he might never witness such an act again. Damn, his wife was sexy. Man-Killer Connaught indeed. She had certainly slain him. And what a way to go.

"I think I'm going to need some help with the rest," she said with a playful little smile.

She didn't need to ask him twice. With one giant step, he covered the scant distance that separated them, brushed his fingers slowly up the length of each of her arms and dipped them beneath the straps of her brassiere. He pulled it from her slowly, and her arms unfolded like a butterfly's wings. Her breasts were kissed with the heat of a blush, their pink tips already tumid with her arousal. He opened his hands over her, palming her, kneading her, but she covered his hands with her own and urged them lower.

Understanding her silent demand, James let himself be led, down over her warm flesh, past the cool silk of her teddy, to the brief wisp of garter below. Deftly, quickly, he unhooked them both front and back, and then stooped to skim the breath of silk off of each leg. When he straightened again, he reached for the handful of fabric still circling her waist, and slowly urged that down over her hips, her thighs, her calves.

When she stood naked before him, her skin fairly glowing pink and warm, James almost rescinded his earlier offer of letting her be the one to call the shots. Because suddenly, he had all kinds of very specific things he wanted to do to Kirby himself.

Later, he promised himself. They had an entire lifetime to explore an untold number of sexual realms at their leisure. And he planned on visiting every last one of them with her.

"Now, I think," Kirby began, issuing her second edict with a warm, wanton smile, "that you need to take the rest of your clothes off."

James smiled with equal wantonness as he skimmed off his boxers and tossed them aside. "Next?"

Instead of answering, she only stood there staring with profound interest at a rather intimate part of him, something that made his pulse rate quicken and his temperature skyrocket. Her interest, like his arousal, seemed to multiply as she covered the final few steps that separated them, bringing her naked body flush with his before lifting a hesitant, tentative hand to cover the hard length of him.

He sucked in a rush of air and squeezed his eyes shut as she stroked her fingers along his rigid shaft, marveling at what a quick study she was. He never would have guessed she was new at this kind of thing. Then again, he supposed that when two people were in love, they instinctively learned a lot about each other, and pretty rapidly at that.

Then he ceased to think at all, because he opened his eyes again to meet her gaze, and fell headfirst into the depths of her arousal. Her pupils were enormous, ringed by pale blue, and full of fire. She closed her fingers more confidently around him then, moving her hand slowly forward, then backward, then forward again, the fluttering of her fingertips an erotic counterpoint to the pressure of her palm. Together, the actions ignited an even fiercer heat inside him, a heat that spread like wildfire to every part of his body. Unwittingly, he closed his eyes again to succumb to the sensation, only to have her intimate gesture come to a halt.

He snapped his eyes open to discover that Kirby was gone. But he located her immediately, kneeling before him, ready to taste him as intimately as he had tasted her the night before.

"Kirby," he whispered on a ragged gasp when he realized her intentions, "you don't have to—"

"I want to." She interrupted his objection before he could utter it, opening her hand over his flat belly. "I *want* to, James."

He tried to say something more, needed to reveal something very important, but the words got lost inside him. Instead, as she drew him into her mouth, he was overcome by a vibration that hummed first in his belly and rippled gradually wider. He dropped his hands to tangle his fingers in her silky hair, stood as still as he could and simply lost himself to her. Utterly. Irrevocably.

Just before the ripples raged beyond his control, Kirby rose, dragging her mouth over his hot skin as she stood, trailing her tongue leisurely over his hard torso and muscular chest. She touched her tongue to each of his ribs, laved his flat nipples, buried her fingers in the satiny hair of his chest. Then she pushed herself up on tiptoe to trace the twin lines of his collarbones, dipped her tongue into the hollow at the base of his throat, then gripped his shoulders to pull herself higher still, fixing her mouth over his.

That, finally, jarred Nash out of his delirium, and he roped his arms around her waist and lifted her from the floor. He spun her around and around as he returned her kiss, then fell with her onto the bed. Together they tore away the spread and blanket, until the crisp cotton of the sheet cooled their hot skin. The reprieve was only momentary, however. Because in scarcely a moment, they were heating up all over again.

James rolled to his back, pulling Kirby atop him, and she stretched so that her body lay over his from head to toe. He welcomed the weight of her, spread his legs so that she could nestle between them, folded his arms over her back to prevent her escape. For a long time, they only lay so entwined, their mouths fused in intimate exploration, touching, tasting, laving, loving. Then he gently moved his mouth from hers, skimming his lips over her cheek, her jaw, her chin.

He pushed her upward until she straddled him, then lowered her again to take her breast into his mouth. She drove her fingers into his hair as he suckled her, uttering sounds of both contentment and arousal. When James finished with one breast, he moved to the other, licking her with the flat of his tongue before tantalizing her with its tip.

He flattened his hands over her bare back, skimming them gradually lower, until he cupped each of her full buttocks in his hands. When he found the soft cleft dividing them, he curved his fingers inside, pressing, prancing, probing, until he heard her moan with delight. Then slowly he pushed her hips forward, moving her up over his belly and chest, until that most intimate part of her lay only inches away from his mouth.

With one final, gentle shove, James nudged her forward, maneuvering his mouth over her, tasting her deeply, passionately, thoroughly.

Kirby gasped for breath and nearly lost consciousness with the new onslaught that shook her. She felt James's hands covering her bottom, pushing her more insistently against his marauding mouth. Instinctively she reached behind herself, locating him, palming him, an action that resulted in a growl of satisfaction before he increased his attentions.

Never in her wildest dreams would she have imagined that she could feel so good. Not just physically, but emotionally, spiritually, completely. Over and over James pleasured her, consuming her, loving her. A shudder of ecstasy wound through her, slowly at first, gradually building until she nearly collapsed at the depth of the erotic turbulence that rocked her.

And then, somehow, she was straddling his midsection again, James smiling beneath her, reaching for her breasts.

"This time," he said, his voice a little gruff, "you set the pace."

And before she could ask him what he meant, he gently urged her backward, lifting her by the hips until she was poised above his ripe arousal. She flattened her palms on his hard chest and slowly began to descend, inhaling a quick breath as he breached the threshold of that which made her a woman. Slowly, oh...so...slowly, Kirby moved herself down on him, savoring each full inch of him as he penetrated her more deeply. James, too, seemed to be overcome by the intensity of their union, because he sighed his delight as he filled her.

"Oh, you feel so good," he murmured.

She nodded, understanding completely. "More," she said simply. "I want more."

This time he joined in, gripping her hips more fiercely, urging her downward as he arched up to greet her. Deeper and deeper he entered her, until their bodies were united totally. For one long moment, Kirby only remained motionless, reveling in the newness of her feelings, in the strange fire that had kindled inside her. Gone was the pain that had marked their first union. This time she felt...full. Complete. Content.

Then James lowered his hips back to the bed, and all she could do was follow him down. Slowly he rose to fill her once more, then gently moved away again. Impatient now, Kirby followed his motions, but little by little she increased their rhythm. He seemed to understand her need, because he, too, stepped up the pace.

That wonderful ripple of pleasure began to unwind in her belly again, expanding outward in a rapid uncoiling of pure delight. Faster and faster, she rose and fell above him, her breathing quickening when he began to buck hard against her. She reached backward to fill her hand with the rest of him, and immediately, he shuddered and stilled. Then in a white-hot burst of heat, he emptied himself into her, marking her, filling her, appeasing her.

And then Kirby was on her back beneath him, her arms roped around his neck, his hand splayed open over her belly, his head nestled between her breasts. Neither said a word as they waited for their breathing to calm and their hearts to steady. Instead they only lay in silence, marveled at what had happened and sent their thanks up to the heavens.

Epilogue

The Galaxy Ball at Mrs. Pendleton Barclay's estate the following weekend brought with it a number of things to celebrate: Bob's departure from even the most telescopic view, the Endicotians' return to normal behavior, Angie's and Kirby's weddings, and Rosemary's engagement. And virtually the entire town turned out to join the party.

Mrs. Barclay's mansion on the outskirts of town, like her boat-house on the river, was a feast for the eyes, one Kirby couldn't help but want to completely redo room by room. The ballroom alone, where she shared a table with her two best friends and all of their recently acquired men—now *there* was a bizarre natural phenomenon if ever there was one—was just ripe for redecoration.

Thick gold drapes, although thrown open wide for the party, spilled heavily from floor-to-ceiling windows that spanned the entire length of one wall. Huge, overdone, crystal chandeliers dangled from a height of fifteen feet, sparkling with soft light now that the sun had set. The parquetry was of a zigzag design more suited to the tacky seventies, and the boring eggshell paint

on the walls simply had to go. Although, she decided further as
she turned her gaze upward, she wouldn't do a thing to the ceiling.

Painted a rich sapphire, the ceiling was gilded with hundreds
of stars that surrounded a playful rendition of the sun and full
moon and each of the nine planets of the solar system...and a
comet named Bob zipping past Earth. Better yet, the artist had
chosen to paint each of the celestial bodies with faces, and now
Willis Random was beside himself with the whimsy of it all.

"Talk about disrespect," he muttered, shaking his head at the
mural overhead. "Whoever painted that ceiling had absolutely no
concept of syzygy."

"Willis..." Rosemary said in a cautionary voice. "You promised not to get all astrophysical on everyone." Then she leaned
in closer and dropped her voice a bit as she added, "Besides, you
know what all that scientific talk does to me."

He smiled, his expression clearly libidinous. "Syzygy," he said
again, this time with a suggestive little lilt to his voice.

"Willis..." Rosemary warned him.

But he only smiled more and added, "Carbonaceous chrondite."

Rosemary closed her eyes, and a bright spot of pink appeared
on each of her cheeks. "Don't...you...dare..."

"Spectroscopic binary," he said further, dipping his head toward her neck. His voice lowered even more as he continued,
"Nadir. Lunar occultation."

"Oh, Willis..."

"Schwarzschild radius. Flocculus..."

"Oooh...Wiiilllliiisss..."

"*So*... have you guys set a wedding date yet or what?" Kirby
interrupted, hoping to rein the couple in before they embarrassed
themselves in front of everyone.

For a moment, they only continued to gaze into each other's
eyes with maddening intensity, then Rosemary seemed to remember herself. "Oh. Um. Yeah. The wedding." She turned her attention back to the table of friends. "Actually, I think we're going
to get settled in Boston first, then come back here in December
for the wedding."

Willis nodded his agreement. "We want to find a house big enough for Rosemary to have a studio. She's about to send her first children's book proposal off to a literary agent, you know. *Petey in the Marshall Islands.* It's riveting."

Rosemary laughed and swatted at him, but he only looped an arm around her shoulder and pulled her close. "We're going to miss you guys," she said, sobering some. "But you know how I've always wanted to travel and see other places."

"You can come home whenever Willis has a break from MIT," Angie said. "And we'll all come up there and bother you guys from time to time. Keep the fridge stocked, just in case."

"Yeah, but seeing as how I'll be starting at Ellison Pharmaceuticals next week," Ethan added in his thick, South Philly accent, "it's probably gonna be a while before I get any vacation time."

"Yeah, right," Angie interjected with a dubious laugh. "You're going to be vice president, remember. Not to mention the fact that your father-in-law is the boss. And I can talk Daddy into anything. Trust me."

"Angel, don't even think about it," her husband warned her. "I wanna start off on the right foot with your old man. Sure, we bought the house up the street from your parents, just like we promised, and I have solemnly vowed to put a bun in your oven or die trying. But nothin's settled yet, you hear what I'm sayin'?"

This time Angie was the one to blush furiously. "Ethan..." she said softly. Quickly she changed the subject. "We'll be needing a decorator for the house, Kirb. I'm clueless about that stuff."

"If I have time," Kirby told her with a breezy shrug.

Angie arched her brows in surprise. "Time? I thought you had nothing but time."

"That was before I got married," she said, smiling.

James nodded as he hooked his arm over the back of her chair and toyed with the lace that edged the big collar of her dress. "Yeah, Kirby and I have plans," he agreed. "We're buying the old Jensen house on Marigold Street. It needs a lot of work."

"That place is huge," Rosemary pointed out. "Do you really need that much room? I mean, I just assumed the two of you would be doing a lot of traveling."

They nodded in unison, but James was the one to say, "Oh, we'll travel. Sometimes. When we can get away with the family."

"The family?" Rosemary and Angie chorused as one.

Kirby smiled. "Ethan's not the only, um...baker...in town, you know. James and I are working on putting a bun or two of our own in the oven."

Rosemary and Angie exchanged knowing glances, then Rosemary turned to Willis.

"Willis," she said, "we haven't really done any talking about pastries yet. How do you feel about buns in ovens?"

Willis smiled back, very salaciously. "Aphelion," he said. "Canopus. Uranometry. Widmanstatten figures..."

Rosemary stood quickly enough to topple her chair and grabbed Willis by the hand. "We have to go now. Goodbye."

And without further adieu, they were crossing the massive dance floor, neither offering a backward glance.

"We have to leave, too," Angie said suddenly, talk of buns evidently striking her in that peculiar way, as well. "But we'll see you guys this week, right?"

"Oh, you'll be seeing a lot of us," Kirby promised. "We're not going anywhere for a while. We have a normal, happy life to lead."

Angie chuckled. "And what better place, right? Especially since *nothing* exciting *ever* happens in Endicott."

"Riiiiight," James and Ethan agreed with identical chuckles.

Kirby laughed, too, as she watched Ethan and Angie make their way in the same direction Rosemary and Willis had gone. She turned to James and was about to comment further, when a conversation at a neighboring table caught her attention.

"Wishes?" a young male voice blurted out. "You guys actually made *wishes* when Bob passed overhead?"

She turned in her chair to glance behind her, and saw four boys who appeared to be, oh...roughly fifteen years old, seated side by side.

"*Shh,*" one of them cautioned the loudmouth. "Will you please keep it down? The wishes may not come true if other people hear, even if we were all born in the last year of the comet."

The first boy shook his head incredulously. "Unbelievable," he muttered. "Just what the hell did you wish *for?*"

James started to say something to Kirby, but she squeezed his arm tight and tilted her head toward the conversation. He arched his brows inquisitively, but joined her in eavesdropping.

"I wished Marcy Hanlon would see me as something other than the lawn boy," the *shh*ing boy replied easily.

"I wished for a million dollars," the second one confessed.

"And I wished that just once, something interesting would happen in this town," the third confirmed.

Kirby couldn't stand it. She had to turn around and offer a comment. "You better be careful what you wish for, boys," she couldn't help saying as she twined her fingers with James's. "Because you know...you just might get it."

And with that, she and James followed the example of Rosemary and Willis and Angie and Ethan. They started off for home to do a little baking.

*   *   *   *   *

Silhouette® Books
is proud to announce the arrival of

A MOTHER'S GIFT

This May, for three women, the perfect Mother's Day gift is mother*hood!* With the help of a lonely child in need of a home and the love of a very special man, these three heroines are about to receive this most precious gift as they surrender their single lives for a future as a family.

Waiting for Mom
by Kathleen Eagle
Nobody's Child
by Emilie Richards
Mother's Day Baby
by Joan Elliott Pickart

Three brand-new, heartwarming stories by three of your favorite authors in one collection—it's the best Mother's Day gift the rest of us could hope for.

Available May 1998 at your favorite retail outlet.

Take 4 bestselling love stories FREE

Plus get a FREE surprise gift!

Special Limited-time Offer

Mail to Silhouette Reader Service™

3010 Walden Avenue
P.O. Box 1867
Buffalo, N.Y. 14240-1867

YES! Please send me 4 free Silhouette Desire® novels and my free surprise gift. Then send me 6 brand-new novels every month, which I will receive months before they appear in bookstores. Bill me at the low price of $3.12 each plus 25¢ delivery and applicable sales tax, if any.* That's the complete price and a savings of over 10% off the cover prices—quite a bargain! I understand that accepting the books and gift places me under no obligation ever to buy any books. I can always return a shipment and cancel at any time. Even if I never buy another book from Silhouette, the 4 free books and the surprise gift are mine to keep forever.

225 SEN CF2R

Name	(PLEASE PRINT)	
Address	Apt. No.	
City	State	Zip

This offer is limited to one order per household and not valid to present Silhouette Desire® subscribers. *Terms and prices are subject to change without notice.
Sales tax applicable in N.Y.

UDES-696

©1990 Harlequin Enterprises Limited

BEVERLY BARTON

Continues the twelve-book series— 36 Hours—in April 1998 with Book Ten

NINE MONTHS

Paige Summers couldn't have been more shocked when she learned that the man with whom she had spent one passionate, stormy night was none other than her arrogant new boss! And just because he was the father of her unborn baby didn't give him the right to claim her as his wife. Especially when he wasn't offering the one thing she wanted: his heart.

For Jared and Paige and *all* the residents of Grand Springs, Colorado, the storm-induced blackout was just the beginning of 36 Hours that changed *everything!* You won't want to miss a single book.

Available at your favorite retail outlet.

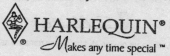

DIANA PALMER
ANN MAJOR
SUSAN MALLERY

RETURN TO WHITEHORN

In **April 1998** get ready to catch the bouquet. Join in the excitement as these bestselling authors lead us down the aisle with three heartwarming tales of love and matrimony in Big Sky country.

A very engaged lady is having second thoughts about her intended; a pregnant librarian is wooed by the town bad boy; a cowgirl meets up with her first love. Which Maverick will be the next one to get hitched?

Available in **April 1998.**

Silhouette's beloved **MONTANA MAVERICKS** returns in Special Edition and Harlequin Historicals starting in February 1998, with brand-new stories from your favorite authors.

Round up these great new stories at your favorite retail outlet.

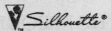